Only-By-Darkness

RUSSELL PROCTOR

CONTENTS

ACKNOWLEDGMENTS

Thanks go to my fellow members of The Very Hardworking Writers Group for their feedback and assistance.

Special thanks to Amy Curran for her help with the final manuscript.

Cover design by www.beyondbookcovers.com.

CHAPTER 1

BRUSSELS SPROUTS FROM MARS

Molly hated brussels sprouts.

When her mother brought dinner in from the kitchen there were good things on Molly's plate: beef sausages and gravy, and grilled tomatoes and potatoes—but there, lurking on the side, were four large brussels sprouts.

The thing was, Molly reasoned, *nobody* liked brussels sprouts. Adults just pretended to, to make children eat them.

"Oh," she said, staring at her plate. "Brussels sprouts."

On the other side of the table, Mum poured herself a glass of water. "What's the matter?"

Molly shook her head and nudged the sprouts away from the roast potatoes so they didn't infect them with their horridness. "You know I don't like them. Uncle Edmund won't touch them either," she said.

"I don't remember that," said her mother. "Your Grandma used to serve them all the time. They're good for you." She dug a fork into one of her own sprouts and put it into her mouth.

And *that*, thought Molly, was the reason adults made children eat horrible-tasting vegetables. They were good for you. Why did good things have to taste bad? Brussels sprouts were weird: small and dark green, like something from Mars. There were pictures of Martians on the cover of a book she was reading, and these brussels sprouts looked a lot like them. She rolled one of them around with her fork.

"Eat up," said Mum.

Molly had a few mouthfuls of sausage and some potato. They

were fine, nothing wrong with them at all. But soon the inevitable moment came when eating a sprout would be necessary, if only to make her mother stop looking at her.

She lunged at a sprout with her fork. Argh! It hadn't been cooked enough! "It's hard!" she said, stabbing it several times as proof. The Martian vegetable refused to be invaded by the vicious fork from the planet Earth.

"I like them a little hard," said her mother. "If you cook them too much they lose their goodness."

Molly didn't know if that were true or not, but put the sprout in her mouth and managed to bite it in half. But she couldn't swallow. She tried to, she really tried. But no good. Her throat tightened, her brain revolted, and before she could stop herself she spat the pieces out.

A bad move. One half bounced off the edge of her plate onto the table; the other, perhaps feeling more mischievous, dropped into Molly's lap.

Her mother frowned, her own fork halfway to her mouth.

"It wasn't my fault," protested Molly. "It just jumped out."

To Molly that made perfect sense, but her mother was an adult, and adults seldom saw how things made sense.

"It didn't jump," said her mother. "You spat it out." After they had chewed in silence for a few moments, her mother added, "So, how are things at school?"

Molly was happy to talk about something other than brussels sprouts, but not so pleased to switch the topic to school. "We have a Maths test tomorrow," she said. When her mother wasn't looking Molly picked up a sprout and dropped it into her napkin. Two down, two to go.

"Have you studied for it?"

Not as much as she should have. Maths wasn't Molly's best subject. But she said, "Yes. I need to do some more tonight. Please, may I be excused?"

Mum examined Molly's plate. "Eat your dinner first."

So Molly ate everything—well, almost everything. She managed to force down a sprout, following it quickly with some roast potato to get rid of the aftertaste. She left the fourth sprout on the plate and hoped her mother didn't object.

She didn't. "You're going to study for your exam now?"

"Yes."

"I'll bring you some dessert soon."

"No thanks. I'm full."

"All right," said her mother.

Molly stood up. "Thank you." She pushed her chair in and walked out of the dining room slowly. As soon as she reached the hallway she hurried to her bedroom.

She hadn't liked the bedroom when she first came to live on her grandfather's farm outside the small country town of Moolooran. It stood separate to the rest of the house, along a short passage beyond the kitchen, a sort of add-on to the rest of the place. The bedroom furniture dated from Molly's grandparents' day and the walls had been bare except for a horrible landscape painting. But once Molly put some of her own possessions in, the room didn't look so bad. Next to the wardrobe with her clothes stood a big cupboard where she kept her toys and books. On the other side of the room sat a large desk where she did her homework. In one corner of the room a music stand had been set up where Molly did her violin practice—not nearly as often as she should. On the desk sat a globe of the world. It had been an eleventh birthday present from her best friend Jess back home, and seeing it now reminded Molly how much she missed her and the other friends she had to leave behind. "We'll travel the world!" Jess had declared, and they picked out countries they would visit together when they grew up.

"But right now I'm stuck here, Jess," Molly said as she spun the globe.

Her mother had grown up on the farm and only moved to the city after she finished school. Molly had been born in the city and had visited the farm a few times when Grandpa was alive. She'd enjoyed it then, but that was because she hadn't had to live there. But when Grandpa died a year ago, Mum had inherited the farm and decided to move back to her old town. And of course, Molly had to go too. It seemed so unfair.

She burrowed in her school backpack for her Maths textbook, but found it hard to concentrate. The numbers seemed all jumbled. It would have been better back in her real bedroom at home in the city. She closed the Maths book and took out her sketch pad and coloured pencils and drew her mother sitting at the table eating a brussels sprout. She tried to make her mother look happy but the expression turned out sour. After an hour of trying to draw, and glancing guiltily at her Maths book every so often, she gave up and went to say goodnight.

Her mother sat reading a book in the lounge room. "Have you finished studying?" she asked.

"Yes."

"What's the square root of a hundred and twenty-one?"

Molly had to think. Square roots weren't part of tomorrow's test. "Um…eleven?"

"Very good. All right, good night."

Molly kissed her mother then cleaned her teeth and went back to her bedroom. There she picked up her book with Martians on the cover. Yes, they looked like brussels sprouts. She turned out the main light, switched on a small reading lamp attached to the head of the bed and lay down. The plastic stars and planets stuck to the ceiling glowed—distant worlds waiting to be explored. But Molly was trapped on this one.

She closed her eyes and tried to remember previous visits to the farm when her grandfather had been alive. It seemed ages ago. The vegetable plots were bare now. The only things Mum seemed interested in growing were flowers, and not many of them.

She opened her eyes again to check the stars overhead still gleamed. They did. At least some things never changed.

CHAPTER 2

WIRE AND WOOD

Molly woke hours later. The stars on the ceiling had faded and the night lay thick in her room. Her mother must have checked on her and turned out the light. Molly hadn't meant to fall asleep like that.

A dog barked twice. Tessa, their Irish setter. Perhaps she had seen a possum or fox that had strayed out from the trees.

The farm lay a fair distance from Moolooran, bordered at the back with a barbed wire fence, beyond which lay the forest. Molly had wanted to explore it when they first came to live at the farm, but it had always been out of bounds, even in Grandpa's day. No one lived there. Mum had reminded Molly on her arrival to stay out of it.

Another bark. The dog should have been locked up in the laundry, not roaming the garden. Molly fetched a torch from the cupboard and padded over to the window. If Tessa was barking at an animal, the torchlight might frighten it away and the dog would go back to sleep. The moon shone weakly, just a thin crescent low in the sky. A few stars easily outshone the faded stars on her ceiling. The large ghost gum in the garden reached long fingers into the night.

Molly opened the window and shivered a little as a soft breeze came through.

"Tessa!" she hissed. "Shush!"

Another bark from the dog. Molly shone her torch on what she thought was Tessa, but it turned out to be just a rose bush.

No reply.

Molly shone the torch around looking for the dog. She leaned out further, her tummy on the window-sill.

Too far!

She put her hands out to stop herself slipping forward, and the torch fell from her grasp. Urgh! Now there were two things to fetch in: Tessa and the torch.

Going out through the back door meant walking past her mother's bedroom and the back door made an awful squeak when opened, especially at night. Everything sounded louder at night. Better, easier, to climb out the window, fetch the torch and look for Tessa. Not worth disturbing her mother just for a possum or wallaby.

She put on a warm jacket—a favourite one she'd received last Christmas—and a pair of sneakers, and clambered over the window sill into the garden below. Her torch lay between two clumps of geranium plants. She picked it up and shone it around the garden. No Tessa. No sound from anything at all, just the hush of the wind under the moon.

"Tessa!" she called again, but not too loud in case her mother was awake.

A flicker of something in the garden, off near the ghost gum. She swung the torch on it but couldn't see anything. When she moved the torch away from the tree the thing reappeared, but again there was nothing to be seen when she shone the torch toward it. Something fast, and small, and only visible from the corner of her eye.

Not Tessa, but some kind of small animal.

Fixing the torch on the gum tree, Molly padded over to it and walked all around the trunk. Nothing but grass and tree roots and fallen sticks. One cracked loudly under her shoe.

Tessa yapped a couple of times. Molly shone the torch in the direction of the sound and there came the dog, long red ears flopping as she bounded up. Molly braced herself so Tessa didn't knock her over, but the dog ran right past her to the ghost gum.

"Ahh!" cried a voice.

Molly looked at the tree, and saw someone running away, Tessa in hot pursuit. It looked like someone the same height as the dog, and thin, with brown hair like a bunch of twigs, and covered in leaves. But when Molly shone the torch on the runner he disappeared.

"Tessa!" she called, not worried if anyone heard her this time. The dog halted at the barbed wire fence. The figure slid under the lowest level of wire into the long grass on the other side and disappeared. Maybe a child had become lost in the forest, and had found the farm.

Arriving at the fence, Molly grabbed Tessa's collar. "Who was that?" she asked. Back and forth went her torch, up and down, but she saw nothing except grass and the first trees of the wood beyond. Tessa sat quivering in Molly's grip, growling softly.

She shone the torch around, letting the beam rest on things she recognised. The old water tank, now rusted and full of holes, propped up on a wooden platform. The garden beds that had once contained lettuces and carrots and tomatoes. The old tin shed which Molly used to hide in, reading books about people having marvellous adventures in magical lands, but which was now full of flower seedlings.

No sign of any child, or any animal.

Maybe it wasn't a child at all. Molly thought of those old stories she'd read. Perhaps the thing she'd seen running so fast into the forest wasn't human: a fairy or goblin or something like that. She was too old to believe in such things, of course, but still...wouldn't it be wonderful if they were real?

Still holding Tessa, she made her way to the barbed wire fence and shone the torch into the trees. The beam didn't go far, the trunks were clustered so thickly together, and yellow grass grew high between them.

What was in there? Her mother wanted her stay out, but the wood couldn't be that bad. With a dog and a torch and a warm jacket, nothing could stop her going at least a little way in and looking for the thin man.

"Why couldn't I see him when I shone the torch on him?" she asked aloud, but Tessa didn't answer.

She touched the barbed wire. There couldn't be anything wrong with just going to the edge of the trees and shining her torch in. Molly glanced back at the house. No lights, so Mum must still be asleep. She would never know if Molly took a few steps into the forest.

What if she met that creature? How do you deal with a goblin? But it wasn't a goblin, another part of her mind said. It was a wallaby or a rabbit. It couldn't be anything else.

The forest trees seemed to lean closer, beckoning her— daring her—to approach.

She lifted the lowest strand of barbed wire and tried to slide under it, but that didn't work. She tried propping the wire up with the torch but it kept falling over. In the end a dip in the ground further along allowed her to slide under with only a single tug of wire on her jacket. Tessa found it much easier and didn't get caught at all.

Dogs were much better than people at a lot of things.

"Come on!" Molly whispered and ran towards the wood.

At the edge of the trees they stopped. The cold wind stirred the dark branches a little, their gentle sigh the only sound. The torch didn't penetrate far between the black trunks.

Beside her, Tessa, sniffed the air and stalked forwards under the trees.

"No, Tessa! Come back!" Molly grabbed at her collar a second too late.

And it seemed then to Molly that the trees again called to her and invited her under their branches. A tingle went through her, a thrill from deep inside. Something summoned her, something dangerous but irresistible. Almost without noticing it, one foot went in front of the other and she found herself passing into the forest. The trees quickly swallowed her up.

Walking was harder than she'd anticipated. The grass didn't grow here, but a lot of fallen branches littered the floor, and dead leaves, and the tree roots were large and always there when she put her feet down. She almost fell several times. When she at last caught up to Tessa she grabbed the dog's collar. "Don't leave me again!" she hissed.

After about ten minutes they stopped. It had become colder under the trees where the moonlight didn't reach and darkness blanketed the world. Molly sat down on a fallen log and scratched Tessa behind the ears. The dog grumbled a little, but kept sniffing the air, seeking the thing she chased.

"If you weren't with me," said Molly, "I might be scared."

Now that she said the word out loud like that, Molly admitted to being a little scared, just a little. Enough to wonder if that that tree over there didn't look a little bit like an old man bent over, rubbing his hands together. Enough to think that the sudden noise behind her wasn't just a branch creaking.

"It's only the wind," she said out loud, but her voice failed to convince even herself. There was no wind here in the depths of the wood.

Tessa growled, and went into a crouch, her muzzle pointed behind Molly, who swung around, shining the torch. The dog darted off under the trees. Molly leaped up about to follow, and stopped when a high-pitched squeal rang out.

"Tessa!" she called, afraid the dog had been hurt. "Tessa, are you all right?"

Another cry.

"Who's there?" called Molly.

A rustling sound came from the leaves at the foot of the tree and then all went quiet. Molly shone the torch around but still saw nothing.

She followed the path Tessa had taken, and breathed out a sigh of relief when she saw the dog standing under a tree looking up into the branches.

"What is it?" she asked. "A possum?"

Molly shone the torch up into the tree but couldn't see anything except leaves and twisted branches. She put her head back so far her neck hurt.

The dog continued to whine and sniff the air, then suddenly

ran off between the trees, her red coat vanishing at a pace Molly couldn't match.

"Wait! Wait, Tessa!"

Her foot caught on a root and she fell forwards, dropping the torch. A small branch smacked her in the face. Her right hand met something soft and squishy.

The sound of Tessa died away and Molly was alone in the forest.

She sat down again, back to a tree, and wiped her wet hand on the leg of her jeans. The torchlight revealed nothing but trees and the occasional glimpse of night sky.

Despite all her confidence on entering the forest, she was now quite lost. Molly turned the torch off to save the battery and the dark night wrapped around her. All sorts of sounds began: movement in the undergrowth, the buzz of mosquitoes, the softest sigh of the breeze in the upper branches. As her eyes adjusted to the night, vague shapes became visible, some of them frightening until she turned the torch on and found them to be a stone, or a twist of bark.

I'm not going to be scared, thought Molly. I'm not.

But she had to think about what to do. If she started walking, which direction did home lie in? If she stayed there, anything might come.

I'm not going to be scared. I'm going to sit here until morning.

A noise to her right: something came at her through the undergrowth. Two bright eyes gazed at her out of a long face, wrinkled and brown, with hair like bristles on top. Molly stifled a scream.

Then Tessa came up, tongue lolling, warm and furry and very, very welcome. The face vanished.

"Oh!" Molly cried. "I'm glad you're back." Courage returned. With Tessa there, all large and red and doggy, nothing could hurt her.

"Home!" she cried. "Let's go home, girl!"

Tessa sniffed the air and headed off through the wood. Molly followed, hanging onto the dog's collar. When they emerged from the wood, Molly sighed with relief. There was the barbed wire fence, and the dark bulk of the farmhouse. Molly scrambled under the wire with care, shut Tessa up in the laundry, and stole across the yard to climb through her own bedroom window.

She shut the window and made sure to put the latch across. If the owner of that weird voice and those creepy eyes tried to follow her, she wanted to be certain they couldn't get in. But she didn't go to sleep for a long time. Part of her feared the face would appear at the window. A more adventurous part of her wished it would. So she lay wide-eyed, staring at the faded stars on the ceiling and listening to the rattle of the tree branches in the night breeze.

CHAPTER 3

THE LOSER TREE

"You're very sleepy this morning," said Mum as she boiled eggs in the kitchen.

Molly blinked and put a hand over her mouth to stifle a yawn.

A school day. And not just any school day, Molly suddenly remembered. The Maths test loomed, and she hadn't studied for it. The memory of her adventure the night before still filled her mind, not numbers and fractions and decimal points.

"I didn't sleep well," she said.

"You were sleeping very well when I looked in on you last night." Her mother drained the eggs and put them in egg cups next to toast fingers. "You didn't even change into your pyjamas."

Molly almost asked if her mother had heard Tessa barking, but that would only raise questions. She felt reluctant to tell Mum about what she had seen and heard the night before, even if she might know something about it. Admitting to running off into the forest in the middle of the night would not go down well.

They picked up their plates and went into the dining room. "You'd better hurry," Mum said, using a spoon to crack her egg open. "The bus will be here soon."

Molly wished grown-ups wouldn't spend so much time telling her what to do. She hit her boiled egg's shell harder than necessary and listened to her mother's guffaw as the egg cup toppled over.

"There's no need to hurry that much."

Molly ate her egg, said goodbye to her mother and hurried to the bus stop just down the road. The school things in her backpack seemed heavier than usual as she climbed aboard the bus.

Students from the primary school that Molly attended sat at the front of the bus and the older kids from the high school filled the back seats. She found a place near the front and put her backpack on the seat next to her to prevent anyone else sitting there.

A few stops later Ava Penfield boarded the bus. Molly winced and avoided looking at her. Ava carried her school bag in both hands while walking down the aisle looking for a seat. She halted for one nasty second beside Molly, then sneered, "I'm not sitting next to you," and turned away. Molly let out a silent breath of relief.

The bus lurched off just as Ava sat down on the opposite side of the aisle, causing her to land heavily. "Ow!" she yelped loudly, looking around to make sure everyone heard, although she couldn't possibly have been hurt.

Although they were in the same class, Molly avoided Ava. Molly actually liked school—that is, she liked learning things. Back at her old school, with her old friends, it would be different. Ava took a delight in pointing out to everyone all the time that Molly came from the city, and therefore knew nothing and didn't belong in Moolooran.

The Maths test went badly. Molly's brain usually went all numb when she saw numbers anyway, but this time her sleepiness didn't help. When Mrs Grey, the teacher, collected the test papers Molly yawned.

"Well!" said the teacher. "So you found the test so easy it bored you?"

"No, miss," said Molly. "I was up all night. Studying."

Mrs Grey's eyebrows came together in a way that left no doubt as to how much she believed Molly.

Ava Penfield handed her paper in with a smug grin.

At lunchtime Molly sat near the Loser Tree at the edge of the playground. It was called that because only the losers went there. The tree looked like a loser itself, with branches that bent over the fence on the far side, as if ashamed of something. To make matters worse, just on the other side of the fence lay a meat ants' nest. It made sitting under the tree a perilous experience—anyone doing so almost always jumped up after a few minutes with a screech, slapping where they had been bitten. A sandwich dropped under the tree one day would be completely gone the next. The kids who weren't losers hung around the handball courts and the playground instead—only the dregs of the school went to the tree. You were either banished there by the popular kids or you sent yourself there.

Molly usually went to the library instead, but today she felt she didn't deserve to be anywhere else but under the tree. Max Henderson, a small, round boy who never had any friends, munched on a gigantic sandwich that dripped blobs of dressing. Meat ants already scurried around his feet snapping up the spill. A couple of other boys who were the brains of Year 6 talked to each other and ignored everyone else. The only other student there was Sarika Jindal, a skinny girl from Molly's class who had waist-length black hair plaited down her back. Ava Penfield once voted Sarika's lunches the smelliest in the school. Sarika sat under the tree a lot.

The day had turned warm and Molly drank from her water bottle, watching the non-losers playing. Her eyes felt heavy and her brain befuddled from the interrupted night and the Maths test. She was worrying about the answer she'd given as the sum of eight twelfths and twelve sixteenths when Sarika said something.

"What?" asked Molly, coming away from the sum with relief.

"I asked you if you're okay. You look…Well, you look awful."

"Thanks," muttered Molly.

"What I mean is, you don't usually look that bad."

One of the Year 6 boys chuckled, but it might have been

something his friend said.

"I didn't get much sleep last night," explained Molly. The memory of those weird eyes and the wrinkled face came back suddenly. She'd forgotten about them because of the Maths test. Now, in the light of day, the forest didn't seem that scary. The thought of some strange creature, a little person, living there, excited her more than anything. She tried to put together a picture in her head of what the creature had looked like.

Sarika spoke again, dragging Molly back to the real world.

"What?" That was the second time she'd said that in two minutes. "I'm sorry, I was thinking of something else."

"You don't have to listen to me." Sarika pulled on her plait and didn't look directly at Molly.

"No. I'm sorry."

"What did you think of the Maths test?"

"Not too good, I guess."

"Me either. It's all right for them." Sarika nodded towards the bright kids. "They have brains."

"You've got brains," said Molly, and tried to think of an example when Sarika had been brainy. She realised she didn't know much about her. "Who needs brains anyway?" she added after a moment, but it sounded really unhelpful.

Sarika's grip on her hair tightened. "You play the violin. I've heard you at assembly."

Molly almost corrected her. She tried to play the violin would be more accurate. It had been enjoyable when she first started out, but the notes still came out all wobbly. Her mother played the trumpet, and played it well. And loudly. The neighbours, who were a long way from the farmhouse, could probably hear her practise.

"You must be good at something," said Molly.

"Mama says I have a good singing voice," said Sarika.

"There you are, that's something. I've never heard you sing."

The girl looked at the ground and flicked a meat ant away with the toe of her shoe. "I could never do that. Not in front of people." She looked up again at Molly. "What's it like in the city? That's where you're from, isn't it?"

Molly wanted to say the city was so much better than Moolooran, but hesitated in case she upset Sarika. Being from the city seemed to be why many students at the school disliked her. "It's all right," she said cautiously.

"I went there once," said Sarika. "It was really cool. Lots of things to do and see. Sometimes I wish…" She stopped and shook her head.

"Wish what?"

"That I didn't live here. In this town. Or go to this school. I've been in Moolooran all my life. I was born here. Can you imagine how sad that is? I wish something exciting would happen."

"I wish that all the time," said Molly. And then she had an idea. "But actually, last night something exciting did happen…"

Should she tell Sarika about her adventure in the forest? If Sarika had lived in Moolooran all her life, she might have heard stories about the forest, might know something about what was in there. "You know that big forest near the highway—" she began.

"Hey! You lot!"

The voice filled the space under the Loser Tree. A leaf fell from the tree as if knocked down by the vibrations.

Ava Penfield stood there, hands on hips, with two other kids behind her: a tall, lanky girl named Katie and a boy Molly disliked more than any other at school. His name was Jack, but in her own mind Molly called him Grumpy because he never smiled. He had greasy black hair and, while shorter than most kids, made up for it sideways. His arms were folded across his stomach.

Katie sniffed loudly, nostrils flaring. The sound of the air rushing up her nose could be heard clearly over the other sounds of the playground.

"So, we have a real line-up of losers today," said Ava. "There's Max the Blob and the two geeks."

Max went bright red and scooted off, chased by the laughter

of the bullies. The two geeks looked at each other as if thinking about running as well.

"And there's Golly Molly and Stinky Sarika," continued Ava. "I could smell your lunch from my house this morning."

Sarika made no reply, but her mouth twitched at one corner.

Molly had had enough. "Why don't you go away?" she said, trying to keep the words coming steadily. Something gripped her stomach and made it hard to breathe. "We aren't doing anything to disturb you."

"Yes, you are," said Grumpy. "You're here." He laughed as if he'd made the funniest joke in the world. Katie and Ava laughed too.

Just then the playground bell rang.

"You can't tell us to go away," said Ava. "This is our town. We don't like people from the city coming here."

"My mum was born here!" declared Molly.

"But you weren't. And that makes it different."

"Why?"

Apparently, Ava had no answer to that. After screwing her face up for a moment, she said, "Little worms like you don't deserve to be here."

"Argh!" screeched Katie. She hopped on one leg and slapped at the other ankle. "An ant bit me!" She picked the insect off. "I hate ants."

Molly didn't dare smile.

"Only morons would sit near an ants' nest," said Ava.

A teacher walked by. "Hurry up there," he said. "The bell's gone."

The two geeky boys scuttled away. Ava looked about to say something more but also strode off, her two cronies falling into step behind.

"I don't like them," said Sarika, holding her hand to her throat.

"They're just bullies," said Molly. "Pay no attention to them."

As they walked back to class, Molly decided not to say

anything to Sarika about what happened the previous night. Best not to tell anyone, just in case word leaked out to the other students and made Molly an even bigger joke. One day, maybe, she'd talk to Sarika about it. Maybe

CHAPTER 4

THE NIGHT VISITOR

Molly awoke in the darkness of her bedroom.

At first, she didn't know if there had been an actual noise, or whether she had just dreamed one. Had her mother knocked on the door? Had Tessa barked again? The stars on the ceiling had faded almost to nothing, so it must be early morning.

A sound came at the window. Rap, rap, rap.

She pulled the quilt up to her chin and stared at the window. Nothing but the moon shining in. Maybe the wind had blown something against the outside, leaves or twigs—except there was no wind.

Another rap, loud enough to cause Molly to sit up. A face appeared in the glass, and for a second she thought it the reflection of her own.

No!

Molly recognised it: the same face she'd seen last night in the forest, the face of the strange creature she had followed, only to end up lost.

Molly should have been afraid, but instead felt more excited. Without waiting to turn the bedroom light on, she jumped up, gripped the window and wrenched it upwards.

The creature's eyes grew even wider. His mouth opened under its prominent nose, but no words came out.

"You!" snapped Molly, angry because she was also a little scared. "What do you think you're doing?"

The mouth closed and opened again. The eyes blinked.

"Well?" demanded Molly.

Another blink. The dull gold eyes weren't normal. They had pupils like a cat, vertical instead of round. The creature was a little thing with a thin, brown neck and skinny body, and although he stood upright, his head only reached the windowsill. But he was not a man, not human at all—not with those eyes, and the thick, bushy hair that stood straight up like bristles. His body looked all sort of crinkly and dry, but after a second Molly realised he was covered in dried leaves stuck or stitched together like clothing.

Her heart beat more quickly—this was something wild and unknown, some strange being out of the forest. A little shiver passed through her like a cold wind, but she didn't back away. Her only concern was that her mother would come in and spoil the excitement of the moment.

"Answer me," she said slowly, "Or I'll…"

"You'll what?"

She tried to think of something horrible. "I'll pull your leaves off!"

The creature backed off a step. "You're not frightened?"

But Molly hadn't been frightened that day when Ava had bullied her at school—not really—and she refused to back down now. "Of course not!" she barked.

"I wanted to frighten you."

"Well that's not nice."

"It's not supposed to be nice."

The moon came out from behind a cloud and the creature faded a little, as if slightly out of focus. Molly could see the garden through his body.

"What are you?' she demanded.

The creature stepped away from the window and spread his arms. Its face twisted into a scowl.

"What do you think I am?"

"I don't know. Something out of a fairy tale, I guess. A goblin?"

The little being hopped up and down in a truly odd manner, almost, Molly thought, as if he had trodden on something sharp. The creature chanted in a deep, slow voice, "I'm not a goblin. I'm a horrible monster come to scare you to pieces!"

Molly frowned at him. "You'd be more frightening," she said, "if I could see you better." Since the thing had stepped away from the window it had become even dimmer than before.

He stopped his dance and glanced up at the sky. "Wait a moment," he said.

A cloud passed across the moon and the night became darker. Strangely, Molly could see the thing more clearly now.

"There!" he cried. "Now you can see me better, you must be even more scared."

"Shh!" hissed Molly. "Not so loud, unless you want to wake Tessa!"

He stopped and lowered his arms. "Who's that?"

"The dog. You didn't seem to like her much last night. I'll call for her if you don't behave." Tessa was locked in the laundry and couldn't get out if she wanted to, but Molly didn't mention that.

The creature hunched down and looked from side to side as if expecting to see the dog come charging around the corner of the house. "Please don't do that!"

"Come here then."

He stepped closer and glared. "Let me be absolutely clear about this," he said. "You aren't scared of me?"

"No." Molly decided he wasn't nearly as fierce as he imagined. "Now, I'm going to ask once more. Who—what—are you?"

He folded his arms and drew himself up to his full sixty centimetres of height. "I'm a wood sprite."

Molly blinked and pulled away from the window a little. Her heart raced and it felt like her insides were vibrating. A sprite! She had read story-books in which they appeared as characters, but they were nothing like this twiggy thing. So they did exist after all! And here was one, talking to her through her bedroom window.

"Really?" she said.

He screwed up his face and thrust a long, twiggy finger at her. "Yes, a wood sprite, and you'd better be careful, because I can be really fierce when I want to."

Before Molly could react, he clambered through the window and dropped onto the carpet. Molly just managed to stifle a cry of alarm, retreated to her bed, and sat down.

"What do you want?" she asked.

"For you to go away," he said.

"Go away? But this is my bedroom."

"I don't mean this room. I mean this farm. This town. Go away!"

Molly had had just about enough of people telling her they didn't want her around. She didn't like it when Ava said so at school, and she certainly didn't like this sprite saying so now. "What's your name?" she asked to change the subject.

He scowled, but answered, "Only-By-Darkness."

The night air had crept through the open window. Molly pulled the eiderdown over her knees. "That's a strange name."

"What's wrong with it?"

"Well..." She couldn't think of any good reason, so she said, "My name's Molly."

He grinned. "That's a silly name."

"Well, Only-By-Darkness is too long for a name. Let's see. Your initials are OBD. Obidee. Can I call you that?"

"If you insist." The sprite wrinkled his nose and jumped onto the chair next to the desk. Molly's drawings and school homework lay spread across it. He tugged at the books and they spilled onto the floor.

Molly jumped up. "Don't do that!"

"I'll stop if you go away!"

"But I can't. Not without Mum. And why should we anyway? We live here."

He picked up her pencil case and tipped the contents onto the floor. Pencils and crayons rolled across the carpet.

"Stop it!"

Obidee poked out his tongue, which was the same shape and

colour as a large blade of grass, and jumped onto her bed.

"Get off there you—you—sprite!"

He laughed, a high chortle that reminded her of Ava Penfield's voice. Not a friendly sound at all. "I didn't expect you to follow me last night. You were lucky to have that dog with you—if you'd been alone you would have been really terrified of me."

The little bit of fear inside Molly rose up again, but she thrust it down. "No I wouldn't!" she declared. You're not frightening at all. I think you look funny." The creature backed off a step so Molly went on. "Do you live in the woods?"

His eyes narrowed. "Where else would a wood sprite live?" Obidee puffed out his chest—that is, his stick-like, twiggy chest looked a little bit less scrawny. "Now you know. So: leave now!"

He hopped onto the windowsill and looked out at the moon. As soon as the moonlight struck him, he faded a little.

"The forest isn't what it was," he continued more quietly. "People came and ruined it."

Molly looked at the forest beyond the barbed wire. "Ruined?" she asked. "It looks fine to me."

This time his laugh was altogether inhuman, like water babbling over stones. "What would you know about that? I've lived there for many years. It's my forest. My home. I know what's happening to it."

"Well, I didn't have anything to do with that, whatever it is." Molly felt a bit miffed that Obidee should blame her for something she had no idea about.

He looked at her. "You might be telling the truth."

Molly could see his bark-like skin, grey and wrinkled like that of an ancient tree. She believed what he'd said about living in the forest for many years.

"Is there something I can do to help?" she asked, wondering what on earth she might be letting herself in for. But the thought of entering a world beyond what anyone else knew sent a quick thrill through her.

"Help? You're human. You can't help."

The moon came out from behind a cloud and the sprite faded once more.

"Why do you do that?" Molly asked. "Why do you fade and come back again?"

"My name is Only-By-Darkness. You can see me in darkness only. In the light I'm invisible. So in the half-light I'm half visible."

"That's a bit inconvenient."

He jumped into the garden, landing beside the geraniums. He sniffed and turned his face this way and that in the night breeze. "I have to go," he said. "The forest is calling." He hurried off towards the barbed wire fence.

"Wait!" cried Molly, but he reached the wire, jumped over it in a single athletic bound, and vanished under the trees. No barks from Tessa. No sound at all, and the only things visible were the white moon and the ghost gum.

Molly stared for a long time at the dark bulk of the forest. It called her, too, in some mysterious way, like it had the night before. All her life, she realised, whenever she'd come out to visit Grandpa, the forest had attracted her. Only now did she understand the feeling came from the forest instead of herself. Questions jumbled in her mind and her heart seethed with a mix of expectation and wonder. Something amazing had happened, and she thought—and deep inside secretly hoped— her world would never be the same again.

CHAPTER 5

HEARD BUT NOT SEEN

Shopping in town on Saturday mornings was usually fun, even with Mum. This was because it meant a trip into the town centre, the only place in Moolooran Molly really enjoyed.

Coming from the city, Molly only had experience of large shopping centres containing many shops and cinemas and food courts. She enjoyed going to those, but often wished her mother would let her go alone or with just her friends. In Moolooran, there were no buildings over four stories high, and while the largest shop was Taylor's Supermarket, it was much smaller than those Molly was used to in the city. But there were many other stores along the main street to be explored. One of Molly's favourites had art supplies where she could buy drawing materials. Occasionally, she and Mum would have morning tea at a café before heading home.

This particular Saturday, they had just sat down at a table outside the café when Mum said, "Oh no. I forgot the bread."

Mum always bought bread from Miller's Bakery rather than the supermarket because they made their own bread and the loaves had lovely hard crusts on them. Molly liked old Mrs Miller, who always gave her a free doughnut, so she said, "Would you like me to get it?"

"No. There's a few other things I need, too. You stay here and I'll be back shortly." She rose and gave Molly some money. "Buy yourself some morning tea." Then she hurried off down the street.

The café waitress came and took Molly's order for a banana

milkshake and a slice of caramel tart. This was more like it: just what she'd wanted to do in the city, be all by herself like an adult. Molly looked along the street. A few kids were with grown-ups. A couple of boys lurked outside Taylor's. One pushed the other in a trolley, narrowly missing a dog. They stopped when a girl started talking to them. It was Ava Penfield, looking more like a teenager than an eleven year-old in denim shorts and a t-shirt instead of her school uniform, and with her hair long and loose. She sucked through a straw on a can of lemonade. Molly was so absorbed in watching Ava and hoping she didn't look her way that she jumped with surprise when the waitress arrived with her milkshake and tart.

By the time Molly checked again on Ava she'd gone and the boys were patting a scruffy dog. Whew! Molly had enough of Ava during the week, never mind on a Saturday as well. Two bites of tart and a slurp of milkshake later she took out her sketchbook and coloured pencils and started to draw.

A minute later a voice at her elbow said, "What's this then? Show me."

Molly looked up.

Ava Penfield stood there, still sucking on the can of lemonade.

"It's nothing," said Molly. She glanced down the street, looking for her mother returning.

"There's a lot of picture for nothing," Ava said, leaning in to peer at the drawing. "Come on, give me a look."

Molly pulled the sketchbook away, knocking it into her milkshake glass. Liquid slopped onto the paper.

"Leave me alone!" squeaked Molly, using a napkin to dab at the picture. On one corner of the paper, milkshake had soaked through onto the next page.

"What is that thing?" asked Ava. "A tree?"

It was a picture of Only-By-Darkness. Lots of brown and grey pencil, a bit of dark green for his hair and his leafy clothes. Yellow cat's eyes looked straight out of the picture. The mouth made a small "o".

"Yes," Molly said. "A tree."

Ava made a snorting noise and kicked the table leg. Molly ignored her and picked up a pencil, which she held poised over the paper waiting for Ava to leave.

"It's a lousy tree," Ava said.

For a most uncomfortable minute Molly tried to draw with Ava looking over her shoulder. Deep inside she wanted to tell the girl to leave her alone, but she knew that would only encourage Ava and invite more comments.

Mercifully, after making a few more disapproving noises Ava walked off. Molly let out a long sigh as she continued with her picture. Obidee's face wasn't quite right yet. It needed more creases and wrinkles. More bark, she thought, and then realised how odd it felt to add bark to someone's face.

A voice spoke. "That's not bad."

Molly glanced up, expecting Ava had returned. But there was no one there. A woman at the next table had her back turned.

"Who said that?" asked Molly.

"Me, dummy."

"Where?"

"Right here. Sitting opposite you."

Only-By-Darkness. Of course, she should have recognised the voice. She stared at the chair on the other side of the table. "I can't see you."

"Of course not. We're in bright sunlight. You think I'd ignore my own name?"

"What are you doing here?"

A soft sigh. "Humans always ask silly questions. I'm here to see you, obviously."

"Do you really like my drawing?"

"Hold it up."

The woman at the next table turned to stare at Molly, doubtless wondering who she was talking to. Molly ignored her.

"Is that really what I look like?" asked Obidee.

"Don't you know?"

"I've seen myself reflected in water sometimes. But there

aren't any mirrors in the forest."

"How do you…" Molly had been going to ask how he combed his hair, but the stiff broom-like brush on his head had never met a comb.

"If I look like that, then I like it," he said.

Molly lowered the picture. "Thanks. It's got milkshake on it."

The woman at the next table turned again and frowned, looking for the source of the voice. "Who are you talking to?" she asked sourly.

"Mind your own business!" cried Obidee.

The woman sat bolt upright. "Now see here—" she began.

"I didn't say that!" cried Molly. "It was…" But of course it was pointless to tell her about Obidee, since he was invisible.

For no apparent reason the woman's tea cup rose into the air, moved across the table and turned over, spilling hot tea into her lap. The woman screamed and jumped up, bumping into the table and knocking the milk jug over.

A chuckle came out of empty air.

"Stop it!" hissed Molly.

The woman shook her skirt, now covered in tea, and glared at Molly. "It's not funny! I could have been scalded!"

"I'm not laughing," said Molly. "Are you all right?"

But the woman stormed off into the café.

"Obidee!" hissed Molly.

Something clutched her leg and she almost screamed as the pinching crept up and an invisible weight settled in her lap. The weight lifted off and the table shook a little. The glass of milkshake rose into the air and tipped up, then settled back onto the table.

"Hmm, that's an odd flavour," said Obidee.

"Don't drink my milkshake!" Molly grabbed the glass and put it back on the table so hard more splashed out.

"I showed that lady, though," said Obidee, his voice coming from the other side of the table again.

"No," said Molly. "That was a horrible thing to do. You might have hurt her."

"I didn't know the liquid was hot!" Obidee replied, but Molly could detect laughter in his voice. He thought it was funny nevertheless. "What was it, anyway?"

"Tea, I think. You really didn't know it was hot?"

"Of course not. Sprites don't drink…tea, did you call it?"

The page of her sketchbook turned all by itself back to the previous page, where Molly had drawn a picture of Tessa. A little squeak from the sprite and another page turned hastily to a picture of the farmhouse with the forest behind.

"You can draw well," said Obidee.

A warm glow suffused through Molly. No one except her Mum and a few close friends had told her that before, and it made her feel better after Ava's nasty comments.

"You think so?"

"Yes. A most intelligent girl."

Obidee wouldn't have said that, thought Molly, if he knew how badly she'd done in the Maths test. But the words made her feel better all the same. She hoped he might make more comments like that.

"I have some other drawings—" she began, when he cut her off.

"I need to speak to you about something important," he said. "There's men from town in the forest, and I don't like them. We don't like them."

Unfortunately, before Molly could ask him what he meant, Ava reappeared, still sucking on her can of lemonade. She didn't approach, but hung at the entrance to the café, watching Molly. Obidee must have been right there on the table between them, but Ava gave no sign of seeing him.

"Haven't you got any friends?" the girl asked.

"My mother's shopping," Molly said, turning back to her drawing of Tessa and picking up a red pencil. She gave a few more lines to the dog's head and then felt the pencil twist in her fingers. It scored a thick red streak right across the face.

Ava laughed.

"No!" cried Molly. Her face screwed up with a mix of anger

and tears. "Don't do that!"

"You did it," said Ava. "You're an idiot."

"I didn't..." Molly began, then shut up. Ava would never believe that an invisible wood sprite lurked on the table between them. "That is..."

"Ava!"

Both girls looked up. A woman, hair piled high on her head, glared at Ava from two metres away. "Stop chatting and give me a hand!" she roared.

The change in Ava startled Molly. The girl slumped her shoulders and took the can of lemonade away from her mouth. "I wasn't chatting, Mum," she said.

"It sure looked like it to me," said Mrs Penfield. "Come on. Your uncle's coming over this afternoon. I've a million things to do and you're wasting time with a friend as usual."

"She's not my friend," Ava said.

"I don't care. Stop being useless."

Ava's face screwed up and she looked about to burst into tears. Molly secretly hoped that she would—it would serve her right.

"Mum..." was all the girl said after what seemed an age.

Mrs Penfield jabbed a finger at her, and Ava flinched back as if struck. "One more word out of you and you won't be going to Lisa's party!"

Ava went bright red and opened her mouth but no words emerged. Silenced at last.

"Now come on." Mrs Penfield stormed off and Ava followed, after giving Molly a sour look. They crossed to a dress shop on the other side of the road.

Molly put a hand over the table checking if Obidee was there—if she couldn't see him, she should be able to feel him. But the sprite must have jumped down again. He could be anywhere.

"You!" a gruff male voice spoke. "I'll have to ask you to leave."

The owner of the tea-shop came striding up, with the female

customer beside him. "You've upset this lady and now you're getting into arguments."

"But—" said Molly.

"No buts. Clear off."

Molly stood on the footpath wondering what to do. A sudden grip on her leg told her Obidee was there and she thought about kicking him away, but that would look peculiar to anyone passing by.

At last Mum appeared with her groceries. Without any warning, a man with a totally bald head and wearing a dark suit stepped in front of her and barred her way. Instead of walking around him Molly's mother stopped and talked to him.

"That man!" Obidee snarled. "The one talking to that woman."

"That's my mother."

"I've seen him before."

"Who is he?"

"I don't know."

Mum said something to the man, who was making big gestures with his arms, as if arguing.

"He comes to my forest," continued Obidee. "He's doing bad things to it." The sprite's grip on Molly's leg tightened and she heard him sobbing a little.

Molly's mother brushed past the man and walked towards the café. The man looked about to follow her, then shrugged and disappeared into a sports store.

"Give me a hand, please," her mother said.

Molly put the backpack containing her sketchbook and pencils over her shoulder and took a canvas bag of bread and pastries.

"Who was that man?" asked Molly.

"Never you mind. None of your business. Now let's get to the car."

They set off down the street, Molly following her mother Obidee pulled at the canvas bag of bread.

"Let go!" Molly cried.

"What's the matter?" Mum turned, staring.

"Nothing," said Molly, and that's how they proceeded to the car, Molly trying to keep a hold of the canvas bag that the sprite kept trying to tug from her grip. He stopped when they reached the car.

"Are you all right?" asked Mum. "You're squirming around."

"I'm fine," said Molly.

Her mother opened the car boot so they could load the groceries in. Just as she started to climb into the car, Molly again felt the tug of Obidee's hand, this time on the leg of her jeans. His voice whispered up to her: "I need your help."

Her mother frowned. "What did you say?"

Molly squatted down and pretended to tie her shoe lace so her head was closest to Obidee. "What?" she whispered.

"Meet me in the woods this afternoon," came the soft reply. "We need to talk."

Before Molly could say anything more, Mum said, "Come on, Molly, hurry up."

Molly climbed in beside her mother and stared out the window as they drove back to the farm. She wondered if Obidee was in the car with them, but he didn't give himself away.

CHAPTER 6

BLACK SUITS AND ORANGE RIBBON

By day, the forest wasn't nearly as scary.

The trees were just trees, and the dark places that had frightened Molly the first time weren't dark at all. The tangled undergrowth no longer tripped her because she could see where to put her feet. Even the sounds were different: the calls of birds and the soft clatter of branches in the slight breeze could be identified for what they were, rather than imagined terrors. Beside her, Tessa sniffed at everything, but didn't growl.

The strange compulsion to enter the forest on the night she chased Obidee remained with her—the feeling that being here was right in some way. But because she wasn't supposed to be here Molly's heart raced a little. She had slipped away after lunch, telling Mum she was taking the dog for a walk, but not letting on where. While disobeying her mother and trespassing were bad things, not knowing why the sprite wanted to meet made Molly curious enough to risk disapproval.

She paused at the foot of a large tree, the roots of which curled a long way out from the trunk. Was this the tree she had sat under two nights ago? Long strips of bark hung from the trunk, like peeling skin. A knot halfway up looked like the face of her teacher, Mrs Grey, in a bad mood.

"Obidee?" she asked. "Are you there?"

She didn't expect an answer, but some other noise, an unnatural one, came through the trees. It took a moment to realise it was only a car—but a car close by, not on the road into town. A car in the forest itself.

She made her way towards the sound, when the engine noise cut off suddenly and left just the bird calls and rustling leaves behind it. Before she quite realised, Molly stepped into a different world. A dirt track cut through the trees. On it was parked a large white utility with an open tray at the back. Two men in dark suits stood beside it, looking at a map. They talked to each other in low voices while one of them, taller than the other, pointed at the map. It was the bald man who had spoken to Molly's mother that morning.

The other man, who had blond hair and was wearing mirrored sunglasses, raised his head towards her.

"Hello there," he said.

Molly knew not to talk to strangers, so she merely nodded and started to cross the road away from the car and the men.

"You're not supposed to be here," the bald man said in a low, slithering voice. "Didn't you see the sign at the gate? This is a construction site."

"She wasn't on the road, Mr Fanshawe," the other man said. "I saw her come out of the trees."

Molly paused on the other side of the road, looking for the best way to go through the thick undergrowth.

"Do you live around here?" Mr Fanshawe continued. He smiled but it looked the way a lizard smiled, no teeth and a wide mouth.

Molly put her hand on Tessa's collar. The men might follow her if she continued to walk away without replying. "Yes," she said.

"In that case," he said, "do you know the owner of the farm in that direction?" He pointed towards where Molly lived. "Her name's Cordelia Travers."

Molly didn't answer. The blankness of their expressions, their formal suits in the midst of the forest, the big white utility, all made her cautious. Tessa stiffened a little beside her.

"No, I don't," she said, and didn't feel at all concerned about telling a lie.

"I want to speak to her," said Mr Fanshawe.

"I don't know her."

Tessa growled. Mr Fanshawe looked startled but didn't back away.

"You can't go through there," he said, his voice now abrupt. "It's a construction site. Go back along the road. You're trespassing."

Molly said, "Come on, girl," and led Tessa in the direction the man pointed until they turned a corner.

"Well, that Mr Fanshawe was certainly the man in town that Obidee didn't like," she said to Tessa. "I can't say I do either." He reminded Molly of her old school principal. He had the same sort of cold voice and only smiled when handing out detentions.

Then Molly saw a strip of orange ribbon.

It stretched between two metal posts placed beside the road. More posts and ribbon led off on either side, under the trees and out of sight. Beyond the ribbon the trees seemed larger, older, closer together, as if they lay in the heart of the forest. A dim coolness struck her, and butterflies flickered at the edge of sight. The ribbon obviously marked a boundary of some sort, and its bright orange colour and the metal posts looked so out of place Molly felt that going further would be somehow dangerous. But almost of its own accord, one of her hands reached out to lift the ribbon so she could duck under.

A man shouted. Molly's hand gripped Tessa's collar again.

Another shout, and angry words.

"Come on, girl!" Molly headed back towards the sound, alert to danger but intrigued to find out what had happened. In a moment she arrived back at the road and the white utility. The two men squatted beside it, staring at two flat tyres.

"Both of them!" said Mr Fanshawe. "How did that happen?"

"I don't know," said the man with sunglasses. "But we've only got one spare."

Both men looked up as Molly emerged from the wood.

"You, girl. Someone let our tyres down. Did you see who did this?" Mr Fanshawe asked. His tie had been pulled aside to reveal an open collar. Pink flesh peeked out, reminding Molly of a pig's skin.

"No." Both men continued to glare, so she added. "I was just off the road back there."

"I told you it's a construction site!" snarled Mr Fanshawe. "There're dangerous machinery. Holes in the ground. You might get hurt."

"I'm sorry. I just went a little way." She pointed behind her. "Just as far as the ribbon. What happened?"

Mr Fanshawe towered over Molly. Tessa gave a low snarl. "I heard a hissing noise," he said. "It didn't register at first. There're many odd sounds in this place. When I did look, one tyre was flat and the other one was going down."

"It wasn't me."

The other man rose and removed his sunglasses. His eyes were dark and piercing. "She couldn't have done it," he said, throwing a weak grin at Molly.

"Well there's no one else here," persisted Mr Fanshawe.

Just then Molly heard the rustle of dry sticks and leaves nearby. She glanced in that direction just in time to see the leaves of a bush moving by themselves, as if something invisible pushed between them.

Something invisible!

"I have to go," said Molly.

"Just our luck." Mr Fanshawe kicked one of the flat tyres. Molly backed off, keeping Tessa between herself and him.

"We've seen all we need to anyway," said the other man. "Let's get back to the office."

"But my car!" Mr Fanshawe kicked at one of the dead tyres. "How are we going to get there?"

They kept arguing as Molly led Tessa away towards where she had seen the bush move. She pushed through, Tessa stalking beside her. When the sound of the men had become indistinct, she stopped and looked around.

"Obidee! Are you here?"

A rustle of leaves in front of her and the faintest outline of the sprite emerged from behind a bush. Obidee's high-pitched chuckle filled the air. "Can't talk here," he said. "Come further in."

Carefully Molly followed the pale apparition of the wood sprite as he led her deeper under the trees. Tessa growled but with Molly's hand firmly on her collar she didn't try to chase the sprite.

After a few minutes the ground sloped sharply downwards and Molly had to let go of the dog's collar to use both hands to stop herself slipping down. The trees huddled closer together and she couldn't decide which way to go to force her way forwards.

"Where are you?" she asked.

"This way, this way!"

Molly pushed between two trees, using her hands to thrust aside the branches that whipped at her body and face, and almost fell as the ground dropped away altogether.

She stood on the bank of a shallow creek. Water rattled over pebbles and the trees drooped above the banks. It was too far to jump across to where Obidee, more visible now under the shadow of the trees, waited for her. Molly took off her shoes and socks and rolled her jeans up. The cold water made her gasp. On the other side she followed the sprite further into the forest. After a minute he pushed through a dense screen of leaves. When Molly followed, her hand went over her mouth in surprise.

A circle of white stones ringed a small clearing, each one just the right size and height for Molly to sit on. The trees behind them had long drooping branches hung with leaves so dense they formed a screen, cutting off the sight of the rest of the forest. The gloom in the bower made Obidee stand out clearly. A butcher bird perched in the tallest tree and gazed down with some disdain.

Obidee sat down on one of the white stones and folded his arms. He looked exactly like a small tree branch propped up against a stone. Had Molly not known what he was she might not have noticed him at all.

"You are in my domain!" the sprite intoned in a voice very unlike his usual one, rich and deep and commanding. "You must do—"

Tessa came bounding through the screen of leaves, the thrill of the chase in her eyes. Obidee leapt off his stone and scrambled up the nearest tree. Tessa raced to the foot of the tree, put her paws on the trunk and gave a few enthusiastic barks. Obidee's voice, his usual squeaky one, came down: "Dogs can't climb! Dogs can't climb!"

Molly couldn't resist laughing. As a hunting dog, Tessa was just obeying her instincts. And while she didn't want the dog to hurt the sprite—one snap of her jaws might break him in two like the stick he resembled—it was also good to know that the sprite was terrified of the large animal.

"Tessa!" she called after a minute. "Tessa, heel!"

The dog gave another few barks up the tree, then retreated to Molly's side, where she sat down and shook her head so her long red ears flapped. The dog thought chasing the sprite a most enjoyable game.

Obidee called out, "Send the beast away."

But Molly needed Tessa to help her find the way back home, and anyway, if the sprite was afraid of the dog, then Molly wasn't afraid of the sprite.

"No," she said. "But I will send her to the edge of the clearing. She'll stay there out of the way."

Molly led Tessa back through the screen of leaves and ordered her to sit beneath a large tree. The dog did so, but not without a small snarl of discontent. When Molly came back into the clearing, Obidee was once again seated on his stone.

"This is my domain," he intoned, but the voice had lost the grandeur of the first time. "And..." He held his arms out wide and turned and waved his hands up in small circles, "it's also my home."

"Is that why I can see you clearly?"

"Yes. Here in the heart of my kingdom, I'm as visible as if in darkness."

He looked larger, more like a branch now than a leafy stick, a part of the wildness. He belonged here, not in town or even in the fields. A thick silence hung over the place. Even the butcher bird had flown off, as if unwilling to break the spell, acknowledging that in this bower Obidee did indeed rule.

Molly said, very politely, "I'm pleased to be here. And I'm sorry if Tessa scared you. She's just doing what dogs do."

"All animals are better than people," said Obidee, "but some animals are better than others."

"May I sit down?" she asked. "It's been a long walk."

Obidee put a hand to his sharp chin as if thinking. "Yes," he said. "You may. But don't disturb anything."

Molly sank down on one of the cool white stones and put her arms about her knees to avoid accidentally touching a bush or blade of grass. A wind stirred the higher tree branches but didn't penetrate the bower.

"I never knew sprites even existed until I met you," she said. "That is, I heard about you…well, about sprites, but never knew they were real."

"You don't know much."

The memory of her horrible Maths exam sprang to mind, but Molly knew that was not what he meant.

"We try to know things," she replied. "But if you don't reveal yourself to us, how can we?"

"Ha! Humans have known about sprites for thousands of years. That's where the stories come from. There used to be quite a bit of interaction between our two worlds. The natives who once lived as part of the land, they knew. But modern people have forgotten us, or call us myth. They choose not to remember."

This might become complicated soon, and Molly didn't feel like arguing. Her mother expected her home soon. "So why did you ask me to meet you here?"

Obidee folded his arms again and leaned back on his stone. "This forest is in danger. Its very existence. Those men you met, they want to cut down this forest."

"What?" Molly felt appalled. "Why?"

"I don't know, but it's right where I have my home. And where the animals live. A sprite has lived in this forest for centuries of your time. We used to live in harmony with the native people: they left us alone, or only took what they needed and no more. But now other people are destroying it all."

Molly felt bad, but found herself saying, "But it's just one road. That's not so bad, is it?"

Obidee jumped off his stone and stamped his foot. "Listen to what I'm saying! They cut down trees! My trees! Trees that birds and other animals live in."

"But we need trees," said Molly. "Even humans do. They help us breathe."

"Trees do many things," said Obidee. "But some humans don't seem to realise that."

"I think they're more interested in money." Molly thought it terrible that people would sacrifice trees just to make money. "Those men wanted to speak to my mother. In fact, one of them did speak to her earlier today in town. Mister Fanshawe. You were there, Obidee."

"Yes. He's the man who built the road. Big machines came through, knocking the trees down. He was there showing the other men what to do. And now there's orange ribbon everywhere, and people walking through in greater numbers than ever before. They are planning something bad."

"But why would he speak to Mum? The farm isn't in the forest." Molly remembered that her mother hadn't been too pleased to speak to Mr Fanshawe. It might be an idea to ask her about it. "So what are you going to do? Move to another forest?"

"No! I can't do that. Sprites are born and live in particular woods. Special trees are sacred to us. I can't live anywhere else. And what about the animals? There are many thousands here, from the wallabies and koalas down to the ants and caterpillars. They're being disturbed." A tear had started down his cheek. "If the men cut down this forest," he said, "we will have no more reason to live."

"But that's terrible!" Molly suddenly thought of all the trees that had ever been cut down, all the forests that had ever been cleared to make way for people, and felt sick that animals and other sprites had suffered as a result.

"People don't care anymore about animals or creatures like us," said Obidee.

"You said they had forgotten about you."

"They know about animals! And yet they cut down their forests! They spoil their oceans, ruin their air. People—modern people—don't think at all except about themselves."

Molly thought this was quite true, but it didn't make her feel any better.

"So why did you let down the tyres on that car?"

"Is that what those black circles are called? I didn't know they would do that. I've seen these machines on the road, of course, but only recently have they come through my forest. Not just small ones like that, but big ones too. They made that road. So I was poking at it—at the tyre—trying to find out more about it, and when I pressed on one part of it there was a hissing noise and it went down."

"That would be the valve, where they put air in," said Molly. "I watched my Grandpa inflate the tyres on his car once."

"Well, I was so fascinated by how it went down, that I did the second one too. Then the men must have heard the hissing. They didn't like it much."

"But—letting down tyres! It's so..." Molly realised that if humans didn't know much about sprites, maybe sprites didn't understand humans either. "That sort of thing might frighten away someone my age. But it isn't going to stop Mr Fanshawe. Something else has to be done."

Molly had no idea at all about how to stop the men doing anything. But she knew she had to try. "Why are you telling me this? Why did you ask me to come here today?" A terrible thought occurred to her: Obidee had brought her here to threaten her, or worse. He had spilt tea on that woman's lap that morning just for talking to her. She stood up. "Please don't hurt me!"

"Of course I won't!" He stood up too and held out both twiggy hands towards her. "Don't be scared."

Molly glanced over to where Tessa lay. "I'll call the dog, and she'll—"

"I mean you no harm." The little sprite shivered and his leafy clothes rustled. "Please—I need to talk to a human. I want to know what's happening. You're the only human I know, and you live on that farm."

"My Grandpa bought it years ago," Molly said. "Mum was born there. She went to the same school I do. But Grandpa died last year and now the farm is hers."

The sprite nodded in a stiff sort of way. Molly wondered where his neck ended and his head began; he looked like a single piece of wood. "I watched your grandfather for years working the farm. He knew about the land and respected it. I spoke to him once."

A thrill went through Molly—her Grandpa knew about sprites! Knew Obidee himself! Did Mum know? She sat down again on the stone.

"He knew about the land and respected it," said Obidee. "A real farmer. But he never saw me, and I never told him who or what I was. I was afraid of people back then. I came to the edge of the trees one day when he was working near the fence and we spoke. He couldn't see me in the bright sunlight. He never questioned who I was or tried to find me. I'd seen the town grow from a few houses to what it is today, and I feared for the woods. But he assured me he had no intention of making his farm larger, of intruding on the forest."

This was fantastic! Molly's Grandpa had actually spoken to Obidee! She wondered how old the sprite was: he seemed more wrinkled and crinkled than before, as if the weight of centuries hung on him.

"The farmer had a family," continued Obidee.

"Yes, my Mum and my uncle Edmund. But they both moved away when they grew up. Grandpa stayed on there all by himself for years, working the place alone. And now Mum owns it. Have you spoken to her too?"

"No. I didn't know your grandfather had died. I remained here in the depths of my world."

Molly thought her mother would have been friendly to Obidee had she known about him.

"Many things have happened over the years," continued Obidee. "The town has grown larger, roads were laid down, cars and trucks rattled along it all day. Other farms were built. People pushed the natural world back more and more. I waited and watched. But now, with people building a road into my forest, which they had left alone until now, I decided to act. I didn't know if I could trust that woman who now lives on the farm."

"That woman is my mother! You could have spoken to her." The thought of her mother chatting like this to a wood sprite made Molly smile. "She'd understand, I'm sure." Then it hit her. "So that's why you came to the farm the other night? To talk to Mum?"

"Yes. But that dog chased me off. Then you followed me. I thought you were trying to catch me, that you must have wanted the road, wanted the forest cut down. I realised the farmer had gone and some other people now lived there. So I came back the next night to scare you away."

Molly thought the sprite most brave to return after Tessa had seen him off. "Tessa couldn't help herself," she said. "She's a hunting dog—it's her instinct to chase things."

Obidee reached behind his stone and held up a strip of orange ribbon. His face twisted in a grimace. He threw the ribbon down and stamped on it with a twiggy foot. "There's lots of this stuff in the forest," he said. "It marks places where they plan some sort of mischief. Perhaps that's where they'll cut trees down first. My trees." He peered at the ribbon. "It's made of something I can't identify. What is it?"

Molly picked up the ribbon and ran it through her fingers. "Plastic, I think."

"What's that?"

Molly could see now how little Obidee understood about people and their world. The road must be a terrible intrusion for him. No wonder he suspected Mum of being part of the whole thing.

"I'm sorry for being frightened before," she said. "I wish I could help. It's Mr Fanshawe you want to spy on—that's the bald man back there with the white car. I know you can leave the wood and go into town. If you're invisible during the day you could follow him and find out what he's up to."

Tessa yapped on the other side of the bower screen. The sound made Molly realise she'd been away from the farm a long time and had to be heading back home very soon. Mum would not take it well if they came home late.

Obidee said, "I don't like town. It's too…human."

"You were in there this morning."

"I wanted to see you." He twined his fingers together and for a moment they got caught as the gnarled digits stuck together like tangled undergrowth. He struggled for a moment to release them. "I'd like to see you again."

Molly felt like her insides were vibrating. Such a strange new world, and destined to become even stranger. A living sprite, and things about her Grandpa she never knew, and big men in black suits. Too much to handle. I'm just a girl, she thought. Just a girl at school and I can't do anything. She pictured herself under the Loser Tree with Ava taunting her, and in class with Mrs Grey handing back her Maths test with a smirk on her face. But none of it seemed quite as real as the ground beneath her and the sky above, and the odd little creature sitting opposite. Somewhere far off, breaking into her thoughts, a bird sang. She looked at Obidee, sitting there on his stone.

"Oh yes," she said. And then, more firmly, "Yes. I'd like to see you too."

Obidee nodded. "Thank you."

CHAPTER 7

A TRICK OF THE LIGHT

Molly thrust her books into her backpack and glanced at her mother, who was making sandwiches for her school lunch. Monday morning was always a busy time: back to school after the weekend, Mum helping Molly to get ready before going off to work herself, and all the usual last-minute things. Molly hadn't dared ask the questions burning inside her, fearing her mother's scolding for trespassing in the forest. But now she was caught up in the rush, maybe there wouldn't be time to scold.

"Mum," Molly said, standing in the kitchen door with her school bag all packed. "Remember the other day?"

"What other day?" Mum sliced a tomato with more energy than it normally required.

"Saturday. In town. A man spoke to you in the street."

"What man?" Then she stopped, the knife clutched tightly. "Oh. Him. Yes, what about him?"

"Who was he?"

"No one you need worry about. Just a man."

"It's just that..." Molly waited until her mother had placed the sliced tomato on her sandwich and reached for the lettuce. "I saw him the other day. He said he wanted to speak to you. But that seemed peculiar, since he already had."

The change in her mother was extraordinary. She slapped lettuce onto Molly's sandwich and twisted the neck of the lettuce bag tight almost as if strangling someone. She turned, one hand on her hip, the other resting on the kitchen bench a little too close to the knife for Molly's comfort. "What did he say?"

"He said—well, he asked if I knew who lived here, and he wanted to speak to you."

"Where did you see him?" Mum leaned closer, and Molly took a step back.

"Um—in the forest."

"I told you not to go there!" She jabbed a finger at Molly.

"I know. I'm sorry I disobeyed you. But the men frightened me. Please, what's going on?"

"We'll discuss this later, young lady," said Mum, thrusting Molly's sandwich into a paper bag and handing it to her. "When you get home from school. I'm very, very cross."

That put Molly off asking if her mother had ever met Obidee. As she waited for the school bus, she wondered why grown-ups used terms like "young lady" or "young man" to children when they were angry. Molly had always been encouraged to develop the manners and politeness of a lady, so being a lady had to be a good thing. But sometimes it meant being bad. How could the one expression mean two completely different things?

On the bus Ava Penfield sat behind Molly and poked her with a pencil all the way to school. Molly couldn't change seats because there weren't any vacant ones. She turned and glared at Ava, hoping to look just like her mother had that morning, but it made no difference.

At school when Mrs Grey handed out the Maths test results, Molly's fears came true. C minus. Mrs Grey had written on the paper: "You must try harder!", which wasn't helpful at all. Sarika didn't smile either when her test was returned.

At morning tea Molly went to the Loser Tree. Sarika was there too, so Molly sat beside her on the narrow bench under the tree's branches. The aroma of Sarika's morning tea overshadowed the flavour of Molly's apple. As Sarika lifted a fragrant stuffed roll out of her lunch box Molly said, "Hello."

Sarika glanced at her cautiously. "I beg your pardon?"

"I said 'hello'."

"Oh. Hello."

"What are you eating?" Molly said when Sarika made no further reply.

"Chicken kathi." The little girl looked at the roll and muttered, "I suppose you think it stinks."

"No. That's not what I meant."

"They're always teasing me about my food." Sarika put the roll down as if no longer hungry. "Once they…" She paused and wiped her cheek. "Last week they said it stank up the whole school."

Molly had no need for Sarika to explain who they were. "I'm sorry that happened to you," she said. Now she thought of it, she could never remember Sarika playing with anyone, just always sitting under the Loser Tree. That didn't seem fair at all.

"We don't have to sit here," Molly said. The meat ants had already started to line up, attracted by their morning teas. "Would you like to go to the library?"

"I went there yesterday," Sarika replied. "They were there too, following me. At least here I can see them coming."

Molly looked at the school playground. Katie and Ava were at the handball courts—not because they enjoyed playing handball, but so that they could tease the younger students who were playing.

"Well, how about we just talk here?" The need to tell someone about Obidee was strong. She opened her mouth, but just then the bell rang for class. They followed the other students into school.

"Now," said Mrs Grey, settling her spectacles on her nose, "we're going to do our science lesson. As I recall, last time we were looking at the importance of trees in keeping the world healthy. Who can tell us something we learned?"

Several hands shot up, but Molly was looking out of the window wondering whether to bring up the subject of Obidee with her mother after school.

"Molly!" called Mrs Grey. "Perhaps you'd like to tell what you learned last time?"

"But I didn't have my hand up," said Molly.

"That's right. You were looking around the room and not paying attention."

A chortle from Ava. Several of the boys in the room also giggled.

Molly said, "What I learned from the last lesson was that trees are very important in maintaining the environment. We need them for oxygen and for…"

She stopped. Was that a faint outline under the window, or just a trick of the light? Something that looked a lot like Obidee. Was he here at school?

"Yes?" said the teacher.

No, just the shadow of the bookcase. But Molly could have sworn something moved.

"For…"

"Why do you keep looking out the window?" asked Mrs Grey.

"She wants to see the trees!" snorted one of the dumber boys in the class.

Molly thrust out her lower lip and tried to ignore the flush of heat to her face. She focused on answering the question. "Trees give us oxygen and provide homes for animals. So people shouldn't go cutting them down for no reason."

A hand shot up. "Yes, Wallace?" asked the teacher.

"Trees also provide wood for building," Wallace said. "My dad's a builder. We have to cut trees down for houses, so people can have a place to live."

"Very good," said the teacher. "Yes, trees are useful in many ways. They provide wood pulp for paper, building materials for houses and industry, and a host of other useful things."

Mrs Grey put a picture of a tree up on the whiteboard and asked the class to copy the diagram into their workbooks and label it. They also had to write notes about how trees turned sunlight into nutrients through photosynthesis, and how the tree took other nutrients and water from the soil through its roots. Molly knew all this already, but copied the picture carefully into her notebook. It gave her an excuse to use her coloured pencils and be a little creative with the drawing. She drew a koala and a kookaburra in the branches just for fun. At the foot of the tree, between two of the roots that were busy sucking up water, she drew a small picture of Obidee.

Something tickled Molly's ear. She brushed it away but it came back a moment later. In flicking at it again, Molly's pencil slipped from her fingers, flew across the aisle and hit a boy called Henry. He grunted and sneered as Molly bent down to retrieve the pencil. "Sorry," she said.

"Idiot," Henry muttered.

Molly went back to her drawing and to check that everything that had to be copied down had been. Henry gave a small cry and jumped up in his seat.

"What are you doing, Henry?" said Mrs Grey. "Sit down!"

"Someone stuck me with a pin!" Henry complained, rubbing his backside.

Mrs Grey quickly silenced the laughter. "Sit down and get on with your drawing."

Henry inspected his seat carefully before sitting, and then he glared at those around him, particularly at Molly. She ignored him.

A movement at the teacher's desk. One of the desk drawers slid open by itself. It kept coming while Molly held her breath, waiting for the inevitable. Pencils, staplers and sheets of paper fell with a clatter.

Mrs Grey turned with a start, as did most of the class. "How did that..." Mrs Grey picked up the fallen drawer and placed it on the desk. Just as she was sorting through the contents the drawer fell off the desk again and onto Mrs Grey's foot. She uttered a cry of pain.

Some students laughed. Molly jumped up and ran to the teacher to help, but Mrs Grey waved her away, a scowl on her face that portended bad weather ahead for the whole class if anyone laughed again.

"Are you all right, miss?" asked Molly.

"Get back to your seat!"

Molly scuttled back while glancing about the room for Obidee. Just the sort of thing Obidee might do—he had spilled the contents of her pencil case when they first met in her bedroom, and let down Mr Fanshawe's tyres. He must be here. She caught a glimpse of Sarika's face: puzzled, a little scared even, but not looking at Mrs Grey. Rather, her eyes were turned to the whiteboard, where a picture had appeared in blue marker, a tree and a pair of beady little eyes drawn under it.

"Look!" squeaked Sarika.

Mrs Grey, smoothing down her skirt, stared at the whiteboard, as did everyone else in the room.

"What's going on?" she roared. "Who drew that?"

But every student was sitting behind their desk. Everyone also had amazed or amused expressions—or both—on their faces. All, that is, except Molly, who had her hand to her mouth.

"Stop it!" she hissed. The words came out all by themselves.

All eyes turned on her.

"I mean—we need to stop this silly behaviour before someone gets hurt!" The words sounded as lame to her as they no doubt did to everyone else in the room.

"Did you write this, Molly? Mrs Grey asked, pointing at the whiteboard.

"No, miss."

"She couldn't have!" Sarika spoke up. "She was helping you."

Molly caught a flash of colour near the door and turned to look at it.

"Don't turn away!" roared Mrs Grey. Then her voice became calm as she continued. "I don't know what's going on with you all today, class, but these silly tricks—and attacking people— have to stop." She gathered the contents of her desk drawer and placed them back where they belonged, breathing slowly and deeply. Her voice sounded a bit calmer as she said, "Now, continue with your drawings."

Molly glanced aside at Sarika and flashed her a thank you smile, but the girl didn't look at her.

Lunch time was no better. Molly again suggested to Sarika they avoid the Loser Tree and go to the library. They both found books and went over to the reading area. While Molly flopped into a bean-bag Sarika sat at a desk but didn't open her book. Her black plait hung down onto the cover. Molly hauled herself up again and stood beside Sarika. "Thank you for earlier," she said.

"For what?" Sarika asked.

"For telling Mrs Grey I didn't write on the whiteboard."

The girl nodded. "I know you didn't." She glanced over at two boys nearby and lowered her voice. "Something else did."

Molly felt a little skip in her heart. "What?"

"You'll laugh."

"No, I won't. I'm not like Ava."

"Well, I saw some sort of creature—or at least I think I did. Something like a small man. But I only saw it for a second or two. It might have just been the light coming through the window. But I saw it pick up the marker and draw on the board."

"Did he look like—well, like he was made out of wood? Covered in leaves?"

Sarika sucked in a huge breath. "You saw him too?"

"Well…"

A voice broke through their conversation. "There they are!"

It was Ava and Katie and the boy Grumpy, who must have spilled his lunch on himself because a large stain decorated his shirt. It didn't make him look silly, just his usual obnoxious self. Each of them carried a book, because you had to have one to enter the reading area.

"Go away," said Molly, who really wasn't in the mood to face Ava or her cronies.

"Make me," retorted Ava, sitting next to Sarika, who shifted away. She opened her book—a picture book about trains, of all things—and idly flipped the pages.

Katie and Grumpy sat on bean-bags. Neither opened their books. Katie produced a sausage roll and bit into it. On the wall above her a sign said, No Food or Drink in the Library.¬

"Come on, Sarika," said Molly, shutting her book. "We don't need to stay here." A shiver of fear passed through her at standing up to the bullies.

Ava rose. "Did you do those things to Mrs Grey?" she demanded.

"No!" cried Molly, suddenly regretting her boldness. "I never left my seat."

"Yes you did. You went to pick up her pencils. I saw you." She stepped towards Molly. "I bet you aimed the drawer at her foot on purpose."

"I didn't! The whole class was watching. It came out before I got there." Why did she have to defend herself for something she hadn't done?

"Are you calling me a liar?" demanded Ava.

Molly knew that Ava was looking for an excuse to bully her further, to blame her and tease her about it. To say anything would only make things worse. She kept silent.

"I didn't see you do it, but it must have been you somehow," continued Ava.

Then, for no apparent reason, she slapped herself in the face with the book.

Katie spat out sausage roll crumbs. Grumpy, a bit slower than everyone else, merely gawked at the sight.

Ava emitted a grunt of surprise, then grabbed her hair, some of which had twisted into a tight roll. "Ahh!" she screamed.

Katie laughed, and this time Grumpy caught on that something wasn't right and grunted.

"Let's get out of here!" croaked Ava, and stalked towards the library doors. "I'll get you for that!" she called back at Molly.

"Quiet!" hissed the librarian at the front desk.

Sarika's mouth had broken into a wide grin. "Why did she hit herself?"

Molly looked around for Obidee, but the bright lights in the library made him invisible. "I don't think she did." she said.

When class resumed after lunch, Mrs Grey seemed a bit

steadier, but her mood was not improved. The whole class stayed alert, not wanting to tap the valve that held back the teacher's bad temper.

Nothing more went wrong until the final bell, and no sign of Obidee. As they left class, Molly tapped Sarika on the shoulder. "Where do you live?" she asked.

"In town," the girl replied. "Why do you want to know?"

Molly thought it might be good to invite her to the farm for a visit. The events of the day needed discussing, as did Obidee. It might be fun if Sarika could meet him too.

"I wondered if you wanted to come over to my place tomorrow after school," she said. "I live outside of town on a farm with my mother—well, it's not really a proper farm anymore."

"Yes, I'd like that," replied Sarika.

They arrived at the pedestrian crossing outside the school.

"I go this way," said Sarika, pointing towards town.

"So do I." Molly realised with a pang of guilt that she had seen Sarika on the bus every day, but had never spoken to her. The Indian girl had always just sat quietly and stared out the window. "Will you ask your parents if you can come tomorrow?"

"Yes, I will." The girl's smile warmed Molly. "Thank you very much."

The girls walked to where a teacher stood with a sign to stop the traffic and let them cross the road to the bus stop. As they crossed Molly glanced up the road for oncoming traffic. Ava stood on the kerb a little way further along. Then, without warning, she fell forwards, right in front of a car. There was a squeal of tyres and Ava bounced off the front of the car and struck the road. Her school bag burst open and books scattered.

Sarika shrieked and grabbed Molly's hand.

Ava didn't move as the car driver climbed out and bent over her. The teacher on traffic duty also ran over. Other students gathered around, obscuring Ava from sight.

Molly and Sarika stayed back, horrified. The thought that

Ava might be seriously injured, even dead, sickened Molly.

"She didn't jump out," said Sarika quietly. "I saw."

"Me too. She was just standing there."

Molly's stomach churned. There was only one other explanation. Invisible Obidee had pushed Ava Penfield in front of the car.

CHAPTER 8

FRIENDS AND ENEMIES

"And it was so shocking!" In her mind Molly could still see Ava lying on the road, her school books scattered, her long blonde hair spread out on the black bitumen "She could have been killed."

Mum dug a trowel into the flower bed, the only part of the garden that grew anything now. The rest had gone fallow, the grass encroaching onto the vegetable plots that had once produced lettuce, carrots, onions, potatoes and, of course, brussels sprouts. "She's in hospital," Mum said. "I heard it from a family friend in town this morning. A broken arm, nothing more—not that that isn't serious enough. Is she the sort of girl who would run out into the road without looking?"

"No." Not even Ava was that silly. "They gave us road safety lessons at the school today."

"They should put more road signs outside the school to warn motorists," said her mother, digging into the soil. "Maybe I should drive you to school and back in future."

To her own surprise, Molly found herself saying, "You don't have to do that."

Mum stopped digging and looked up sharply. "Well there's no need to throw out the idea so quickly." A smile broke out. "Don't worry. I trust you."

It was good to see her mother smile. Molly had escaped being told off for trespassing in the forest. The awful news of Ava's injury had driven the idea right out of her mother's head, and Molly had no desire to remind her.

They worked together for a few minutes in silence, transferring some flower seedlings from a plastic tray to the soil, but something kept playing on Molly's mind. "Mum…"

Her mother put down her trowel, but the smile still remained on her face. "I know that tone. You're about to ask me something, but you're unsure of what my answer will be."

Was it that obvious? "Did Grandpa ever say anything about the forest?"

"What forest?"

Molly pointed at the trees looming above the house. "That one."

"A few things. Around here it's called Hallow's Choice, but the Aboriginal people called it something else, long before Europeans arrived. It's been there since long before the farm. Thousands of years, I expect." The smile twitched a little. "I told you not to go in there."

"I know. I'm sorry. Did you ever go in?"

Her mother picked up the trowel again and dug for a minute in silence. Then, "Yes. Your uncle Edmund took me in once when I was very little, and I went in myself a few times. But your Grandpa caught me and gave me a stern lecture and told me never to go in again."

"What was it like?"

"Like?" Mum brushed a fly off her nose. "Like any forest, I guess: lots of things to trip over. Too many insects." Then, after another moment of thought, she added, "It was quiet, I remember that. In the heart of it, you couldn't hear anything from outside. Your own private world."

"Someone's built a road through it."

Her mother's face darkened. "Really? Well…" She sighed. "Hand me those seedlings, please."

Molly passed them over. "Did Grandpa ever go in?"

"I don't know. I guess—he grew up here, so as a little boy he must have been curious. Why are you asking?"

Molly thought hard as she handed her mother another seedling from the plastic tray at her feet. Did she dare ask her mother about anything Grandpa might have said about Hallow's Choice? Could she make a hint without being too obvious? Grown-ups—her mother in particular—didn't seem to like some personal questions.

"You just seem keen I don't go in there, that's all," she said at last.

"Hmm."

After a few more moments of working, Molly said, "How could I find out more about the forest?"

"Well—there's the Moolooran Town Council. They're the people who run the area. There must be some sort of history of the place. Or the local library." Mum looked at her watch. "Goodness, it's five o-clock already. Your friend Sarika's coming over for tea."

Sarika's parents had given her permission to come to dinner. That had been her mother's suggestion when Molly mentioned the possibility of a visit. "I'm glad you're making friends," she had said. "It's been almost a whole school term you've been going there and I've never seen you with anyone."

Tessa barked.

Mr Fanshawe stood at the front gate in his black suit. He held a briefcase and wasn't smiling. His eyes were hidden behind his sunglasses. Mum clutched her garden trowel almost like a dagger as she walked to the gate to speak to him. Tessa stood nearby, ears forward, alert to the stranger. Molly followed her mother but hung back a couple of metres from Mr Fanshawe.

"I've told you before," Mum said, "you're wasting your time."

Mr Fanshawe's sunglasses hid whether he recognised Molly or not. He said to her mother, "Ms Travers, almost everyone else along the highway has signed."

"Who?" She pointed to the property on the right. "I know Clive Drummond hasn't. He told me yesterday." She pointed in the other direction, this time with the trowel. "And the Sinclairs only just moved in. They wouldn't sign away a farm they just bought."

Molly didn't understand grown-up problems. They almost always sounded boring. But something in her mother's voice made a tightness in Molly's chest, and Mr Fanshawe looked as creepy and unforgiving as he had the first time.

"Please leave my property," said her mother. As if on cue, Tessa emitted a loud yap.

Mister Fanshawe stiffened, and pushed his sunglasses further back on his nose. "The Council will acquire the property anyway," he said. "And at much lower cost. You're a fool to hold out."

That did it. No one called her mother a fool. Molly stalked towards the man and growled, "Leave my mother alone."

He looked at her, this time over the top of his sunglasses so his eyes glared. His brow gleamed with sweat. "This is nothing to do with you, missy. I'm talking to your mother."

"Well I'm talking to you!"

The man straightened up and smiled coldly. He ignored Molly and spoke to her mother again. "The Council will apply for resumption. You know you don't stand a chance in court."

Before either could reply, he climbed into his car and drove off.

Molly asked, "Who was that?"

Her mother didn't answer, just heaved a great sigh.

"Mum?"

The trowel shook in her mother's hands. "Did he frighten you, Molly?"

"No—well, a little. Who is he?"

"Come inside with me, please," said her mother, and they went into the house, the gardening forgotten. Trowel and all, Mum sat at the dining table and indicated for Molly to join her. "There's something I need to tell you," she said.

Molly found she was still wearing her sunhat indoors, so she removed it and sat opposite her mother. Tessa plopped down in the middle of the lounge room, as if expecting to join in the conversation. Everything became very quiet except for the laboured sound of her mother breathing, as if she were about to burst into tears.

"There's a company," Mum said eventually. "A big company called Fanshawe Enterprises. They're a construction company—houses, office blocks. They build anything. Mister Fanshawe is the head of it. The Moolooran Town Council owns Hallow's Choice. But they want to buy my farm, too, and all the properties along here. They don't just want the forest, they want everything this side of the highway."

"Why?" asked Molly, as she scrunched up the brim of her sunhat. The cloth felt rough under her damp fingers. This was what Obidee had mentioned—and her mother had known all along!

"So they can turn it into a housing estate there. Moolooran is getting bigger, and needs more land," continued her mother. "The Council wants to cut down all the forest and build houses."

A sharp pang went through Molly. Cut down the whole forest! So that's why the men were there with their map, and why Obidee was so upset with them. It wasn't just about building a road; the whole forest, and all the animals that lived there—and Obidee—were in jeopardy.

"But if the forest is cut down the animals won't have anywhere to live," she said, remembering her talk with the sprite in his bower.

"Never mind the animals!" cried Mum. "They want my house too. And Mr Drummond's. And everybody's. Where will we live?"

"The forest is on a huge bit of land," said Molly. "It's big enough for any number of houses."

"That's the thing," said Mum. "They want to build any number. They want all the land between here and the hills, and the road in front here leads straight to town. It would increase the value enormously." She looked at Molly. "Mr Fanshawe's been hassling me for weeks now, trying to get me to sell. You see? His company has the contract to build the estate. The more houses he builds, the more money his company makes."

"Well, don't sell," said Molly. "He can't make you."

"That's just it. He can't, but the Council can. There's a process called resumption. The government can take any land they want off people, even if they own it. They have to pay for it, of course, but the price is never what owners could get if they sold privately."

Molly frowned. "How can they do that, take people's land away? It was Grandpa's, and now it's yours. It's not their land."

"But they can." Her mother clutched her throat. "I know it's very unfair, but the Council can do it. I checked with my lawyer. He said there's nothing we can do. If we object to the resumption the Council will take us to court and we would lose anyway, and have to pay for the court hearing. It's the law."

Molly thought it was just about the unfairest law she'd ever heard of.

"But what happens to you?" Molly reached out and took her mother's hand.

"Me? I have to buy another house somewhere, and that will cost more than the Council will pay for this one. And I'll lose the farm."

The farm had never been a great money-maker. Grandpa had only ever grown a few vegetables on it, enough for a bit of money but nothing more. But it had been the family's pride and joy, and while Mum didn't show any interest in growing vegetables, she loved the farm.

"We have to do something," Molly said. "What do Mr Drummond and the Sinclairs think?"

"Mr Drummond's against it, of course," said Mum. "But in the end he can't do anything more than I can. I haven't spoken to the Sinclairs yet."

"There must be something," said Molly, as she remembered how upset Obidee was about it. But what could she do to help? Obidee had shown his way of solving problems by letting down people's tyres and maybe even shoving Ava under a car. That wasn't going to work. Nevertheless, she felt a strong desire to speak to the sprite about it.

Tessa barked and a moment later the doorbell rang. The dog jumped up and went to the door, growling a little. Mum, still clutching her trowel, looked up in surprise. Molly, too, felt a twinge of anxiety. Perhaps Mr Fanshawe had come back with more demands and threats.

Her mother opened the door. A tall woman in a bright dress stood there, holding the hand of a small, long-haired girl, also wearing a highly-coloured, sweeping garment that looked so gorgeous and silky that for a moment Molly didn't recognise her.

"Sarika!" she cried.

But not the plain Sarika from school. No one, not even Ava, would call this Sarika plain. Her face glowed and her hair had been tied back in an elaborate arrangement that set off her dark eyes.

The woman smiled and nodded. "Hello. Ms Cordelia Travers?"

"Yes," said Mum, the catch in her breath revealing how overwhelmed she was, too, at the sight of these two splendid ladies on her doorstep.

"I am pleased to meet you," the woman said. "I am Mrs Jindal, and this is my daughter Sarika."

"Hello. And do come in." Mum shooed Tessa out of the way and ushered the two inside. Molly couldn't take her eyes off Sarika. It seemed a pity the school wouldn't let her dress like this.

"I'm not staying," Mrs Jindal said. "I'm just dropping Sarika off and then visiting a friend nearby. I'll collect Sarika in a couple of hours."

After Mrs Jindal left Molly grabbed Sarika's hand and led her to her bedroom to talk.

Sarika cast her gaze around the room, her hands held to her chin. "I love your room!" she gasped. She spun the globe on Molly's desk, and ran her hands over the pink and purple quilt. "You have very nice things."

Molly glowed, and said, "I'm sure you have interesting things yourself. I love your dress."

"It's called a sari," the girl replied, and turned around like a model to show. She wore the sari over a short tunic and had sandals on her feet. "I like wearing it, but we only do so on special occasions."

Molly flushed at the idea that Sarika thought coming to visit her was a special occasion.

"I wish I could wear something like that." She looked down at her own clothes, which now seemed very drab, and had soiled knees from digging in the garden. To change the subject, she said, "The forest is just out the window."

The trees glowed in the afternoon sunshine, the yellow grass partly hiding the barbed wire fence. A soft breeze blew through the open window to raise Molly's hair a little. Sarika's hair, in its tight plait, didn't move. But the smile on the girl's face made Molly wish they could be friends for a long time.

"Have you been into the forest?" Sarika asked.

"Yes—but we're not supposed to go there. It doesn't belong to us."

Sarika nodded, but didn't take her eyes off the trees. The smile went away from her face. "The other day," she said, her voice a mere whisper, as if talking to herself. "In class. I thought I saw…"

"Yes?" Molly felt her stomach tighten a little.

"I told you I saw something drawing on the whiteboard," continued Sarika. She turned her back on the window and stared directly at Molly.

"Yes, and you said he looked like a small man."

The girl's eyes went wide. "Yes. A small man covered in leaves. I thought it was a ghost. It must have pulled out the desk drawer too, and dropped it on Mrs Grey's foot. Ghosts attack people. I was scared." Her voice shook a little. "I told my father but he said that ghosts are only folklore, tales made up to frighten people." She looked directly into Molly's eyes. "What do you think?"

The tight hand that gripped Molly's heart didn't let go, just squeezed harder. So Obidee had been in the classroom. Maybe he had pinched Henry for calling Molly an idiot, and made Ava slap herself with the book in the library. But although she'd been nasty to Molly, Ava didn't deserve being shoved in front of a car.

"What you saw…" she began, and stared out at the forest. "What you saw was real. I know him. Only he's not a ghost. He's been alive for many years. His name's Obidee—well, that's what I call him. His real name is Only-By-Darkness. He's a sprite. A sort of wood-being."

To Molly's relief Sarika didn't show any sign of not believing her. She had half-expected the girl to laugh or call her silly. But Sarika's deep eyes glistened as she nodded her head. "I have heard of such things. In story books. But you have actually met him?"

"Yes," said Molly. She picked up her sketch book and showed Sarika the drawing she'd made of Obidee. "Is that what you saw?"

The girl put a hand over her mouth. "Yes. I think so. I couldn't quite see him."

"That's because he's invisible in the light. But in the dark, he can be plainly seen."

Sarika rubbed her fingers over the drawing. "So life-like."

Quickly Molly explained all she knew about Obidee, and about how she wanted to help him. At the end of her story, they both sat down on the bed, and said nothing for a while.

"What are you going to do?" asked Sarika eventually.

"I don't know." Molly looked out at the forest, her stomach tightening at the sight of the tangled trees and the spiky, yellow grass. The barbed wire fencing it off looked too frail now to hold out whatever dark secrets lay within.

"What if he comes here again?" asked Sarika.

"I hope he doesn't."

CHAPTER 9

TWO DETECTIVES

Molly felt better at school now. Ava had returned, her arm in a sling, but she left Molly and Sarika alone—which meant that Katie and Grumpy also didn't bother them. Each break Molly would play or talk with Sarika, and they became even closer friends. Sarika always had interesting things to eat, some of which Molly found too hot for her taste, but she enjoyed the experience. Sarika loved to look at Molly's drawings, and envied her ability. One day Molly heard Sarika quietly singing while they waited for the bus home.

"That's lovely," she said. "What is it?"

"An Indian folk song. But I don't do it too well."

"Don't be silly! You should sing at the school concert,"

Sarika shook her head so that her long plait flicked her shoulders. "I could never do that. I'd be too embarrassed."

Molly felt this was silly, especially as she had to be in the concert herself as part of the school orchestra, playing her violin badly in a piece called the "Trumpet Voluntary". Molly sure hadn't volunteered for it.

There was no sign of Obidee, and Molly had mixed feelings about this. While she remained appalled at the idea that Obidee had actually tried to kill Ava simply for being a bully (although, admittedly, the bullying had stopped), deep down inside she feared for the sprite's problems with Mr Fanshawe's company. Not just the sprite, but the animals that lived there as well. How could people be so uncaring? She had not returned to the forest, nor had there been any more sign of Mr Fanshawe.

They caught the bus to go home. Part of its route went through town, where Sarika usually disembarked, before diverting round the dam and along the highway past her mother's farm. Just as the bus pulled up at Sarika's stop, Molly noticed Mr Fanshawe's big white utility parked in the street.

She grabbed Sarika's arm. "Look!"

"What?" Sarika asked, about to step off the bus.

No time to explain. Molly grabbed her backpack and followed Sarika off.

"What are you doing?" asked Sarika. She slipped her own backpack over her shoulders. It almost doubled her size.

"That car!" hissed Molly. "That's *the* car! The one Obidee let the tyres down on."

Sarika didn't ask Molly if she was sure. She just nodded and said, "All right. So what are you doing getting off with me? Do you have shopping to do?"

Molly looked at her watch. Four o'clock. The next bus came in twenty minutes, and another twenty minutes after that. She would make up some story for Mum about wanting to spend time with Sarika on the way home from school—or better yet, she'd buy her mother a box of chocolates to cheer her up. That would be an excuse for getting off the bus in town.

"I want to see that Mr Fanshawe again," she said to Sarika. "I'm going to wait and see if he comes back."

"Why?"

Why indeed? Molly had no idea what might happen. She just knew that keeping tabs on the mysterious man in the dark suit was important. A strong urge came to let his tyres down, but there were too many people walking by.

A reason came to her: "I want to know what he's up to," she said. "Obidee doesn't understand people, so we need to learn all we can."

"We?"

"Yes. Don't you want to help?"

Sarika glanced along the street towards her house. "All right. But we can't take too long. You pretend to be a detective and

I'll be your sidekick."

Molly almost replied that they weren't playing a game, but thought Sarika might take that the wrong way and leave, and Molly desperately wanted her to stay.

They walked a few paces along the street and stood outside Miller's bakery where they could keep an eye on the car without being too obvious. Sarika watched the car for a minute or two, then turned to examine the wares in the bakery window. The smell of the sweet buns and sausage rolls and apple slices made Molly's stomach growl; if they went in and Mrs Miller was there they might both score a free doughnut. But she steadfastly remained staring at the car—if they went in, they might miss Mr Fanshawe.

People walked past and Molly checked each one, but none were Mr Fanshawe or anyone in a dark suit. For some reason she expected anyone who knew him to be wearing the same black suit. The car was parked outside a building which had a sign reading Moolooran Town Council, and she kept her eye on the doors to that, too, in case he'd gone in there.

But the minutes dragged by, with Molly often checking her watch. This was ridiculous. Mr Fanshawe might not be back for ages. Adults didn't have to be home by a certain time, didn't have mothers waiting for them. Mum might come looking for her, and her anger on finding Molly traipsing about town on a fool's errand would not be placated by a box of chocolates.

Just as she was about to give up—after a good fifteen minutes—she nudged Sarika in the ribs. The girl emitted a short squeak.

"Look who's there!"

Ava Penfield stopped beside the car and put her school bag down. Molly now recalled Ava hadn't been on the bus that afternoon, and while she normally got off at the same stop as Sarika, surely she would have gone straight home?

A minute later Mr Fanshawe walked out of the Town Council, putting on his sunglasses. In one hand he held a briefcase. He saw Ava, waved and smiled and said something, then dug into his pocket for his keys. As he opened the car door he spotted a piece of paper stuck under the windscreen wiper. He glanced at it, scrunched it into a ball and threw it in the gutter. He then climbed into the car. Ava got into the passenger seat beside him and they drove off.

Molly found she'd been holding her breath.

Ava Penfield knew Mr Fanshawe! They were probably relatives—was he the uncle her mother had mentioned that time Ava had been teasing Molly at the café?

"Come on!" she said, and tugged on Sarika's arm.

"What?" the girl protested. "Are we following him?"

"No, silly!" Molly picked up the paper Mr Fanshawe had thrown away. It was a pink ticket. At the top was the name of the Council, and under that the heading *Parking Offence Notice*.

The gutter was painted with a yellow line. Molly knew you weren't allowed to park on yellow lines.

So Mr Fanshawe was the kind who threw away parking tickets. Only people who didn't respect the law did that—or people so rich they didn't care about paying fines.

"That was fun," Sarika said, but didn't sound convincing. "I'd better go home now."

"Not yet." Molly ignored the frown on her friend's face. "We have to find out what's in this building."

"Why?" Sarika looked at her own watch. "Mama is waiting for me."

"Just for a minute. I thought you were my sidekick?"

"All right," said Sarika, and slipped off her backpack to dig into it and pull out a small notebook and a pencil. "I'll take notes."

"Good idea."

"But if I get into trouble for being late home, I'll never speak to you again."

The Council building didn't look anything special, an office block several stories high, one of the oldest in town. Four stone steps led up to swinging glass doors. The two girls walked in, to find an enormous tiled room with counters surrounding three sides. Stairs led up to the next level. In the middle of the room was a large table, and on it a model of the surrounding countryside made out of cardboard and plastic and placed under a glass cover. The town nestled in the middle of the model. The dam was a large blue area. Grey-painted roads fanned out from the centre of the town. One of them passed a small square of cardboard that Molly realised must represent her mother's farm. The forest was a jumble of miniature dark green trees behind it. Molly thought the model a lovely piece of work, skilfully put together. A pity that people like Mr Fanshawe wanted to change the way the countryside looked.

Several people stood behind the counters serving customers. No one paid any attention to the two girls.

"Over here," Molly said, moving towards a counter fronted by glass with a sign reading *Enquiries*. Behind the counter, a woman sat working at a desk, spectacles on her nose.

Molly waited for a few moments but the woman ignored her. "Excuse me," she said.

The woman looked up, startled, then noticed the girls' heads above the counter.

"Oh, I'm sorry, I didn't see you two there."

Now she had the woman's attention, Molly wondered what on earth to say. She could hardly ask what Mr Fanshawe had been doing there. After a moment, she said, "I'd like to know about the housing development out at the forest, please. The one along the highway."

"Hallow's Choice. Yes, what about it?"

"Well…" What did you ask about housing developments? Molly paused again, feeling rather foolish.

It was Sarika who spoke up brightly and said, "We're doing a school project."

"Yes," chimed in Molly. "About the Council."

"And we want to know how the development is going," continued Sarika.

The woman pushed her glasses higher on her nose. "I see. Well, there's quite a lot of information about that. Can you be more specific?"

Molly felt her face flush as she realised she knew almost nothing at all about the project. She sifted through her memory for the name of the company. "Fanshawe Enterprises," she said.

"Do you have any information about them?" Sarika jumped in again. "Brochures? Or documents? You see, we need to gather as much information as we can and present it to the class." She flashed a sugary smile.

The woman said, "We do have some brochures—but not about the company, only about the project itself. You'd have to ask the company for more information."

"Thank you," said Sarika very politely, and the woman smiled back.

"Give me a minute." The woman went to a metal filing cabinet and started pulling out papers.

Molly glanced again around the room. So this was where the Mayor had his office and the local authority met to discuss things like cutting down forests.

Two men came down the stairs. Molly recognised one from his picture in the local paper— the Mayor of Moolooran. Big and stocky, with slick black hair, he had an air of authority about him. He spoke to the other man as they walked to the front doors.

Molly gulped. Here was her chance to ask the Mayor directly about what he planned to do with her mother's farm, but she held back from interrupting him. Why would such an important man listen to a little girl? He would just laugh, or more likely not even acknowledge her at all. Important people did that, too busy to pay attention to a child.

But her feet seemed to move of their own accord and Molly found herself stepping towards him just as he reached the middle of the room. She wondered what on earth she was going to say. A whole swarm of butterflies launched in her stomach and fluttered about.

"Excuse me," was all that came out when she finally reached

him.

But the Mayor didn't hear her tiny squeak. He and the other man kept walking determinedly towards the front doors and exited into the street. She stared after them forlornly.

"Molly!" Sarika's words broke through.

The woman had returned with a sheaf of papers in her hand.

"Oh. I'm sorry." Molly scuttled back to the counter feeling rather foolish.

"I found some material for you," said the woman. "All about the Hallow's Choice project. I must say it's good to see two young girls taking an interest in local development."

The brochures and other papers covered the counter-top. One paper was headed *Press Release*. Other papers had maps and diagrams. Lots of reading there, and maybe, Molly hoped, some idea of how to stop it all going ahead.

"Thank you," said Molly and Sarika at exactly the same time, which made Sarika giggle.

"Who was that man you spoke to?" she asked as they left the building.

"*Tried* to speak to," Molly corrected. "He's the Mayor of Moolooran. "But he didn't hear me. I was going to..."

What had she been going to do? Beg him not to cut down the forest? Small chance of him agreeing to that.

"What do we do next?" asked Sarika as they walked back to the bus stop.

"Well, we need to look at these papers first. Then..." Now they were no longer in the big, imposing Council building hall surrounded by uncaring adults, Molly could think straight again. "Maybe we could get a committee going at school. 'Stop Hallow's Choice' or something. Can you come to my place this weekend?"

"I'll try," said Sarika. "I made some notes, by the way." She held up her notebook. Neat black handwriting covered the page. "I wrote down everything the woman said."

"But she didn't say much."

Sarika sighed. "I know. But there might be something."

They parted at the bus stop. Sarika went home and Molly boarded the bus feeling rather excited, wondering what the brochures would say, but also uncertain. Ava must be related to Mr Fanshawe. Was that going to make things even more difficult at school?

Just as she walked into the house, Molly realised she'd completely forgotten to buy her mother a box of chocolates. Her mother was sitting at the kitchen table. She hardly looked up as Molly walked in. There were no questions as to why she was late home from school, and hardly any recognition at all.

On the table was a large yellow envelope with the Moolooran Town Council crest on it. An official looking-letter lay open beside it.

"What's that?" asked Molly.

Her mother looked at her. "I'm afraid it's bad news. The Council did what that Mr Fanshawe warned me about." She picked up the letter. "This is a notice of resumption. It means the Council is acquiring the farm. I have to sell it to them."

CHAPTER 10

MAKING A STAND

Mrs Grey looked at the class list and then up at the students ranged before her. Some slunk down a little in their seats, not wanting to be picked. Molly sat straight enough, but felt a small flutter in her stomach when Mrs Grey's finger pointed at her.

"Molly Travers," said the teacher. "You've been living here in Moolooran for a few months now. We'd like to hear about what you think of the place."

Molly nervously walked to the front of her class, thinking carefully. Like most of the students, she found Impromptu Speaking a chore. Mrs Grey would give a student a topic, then have them stand in front of the class and talk for two minutes. Some just stood there and gaped, eyes blinking like an owl's. Some—of course, Ava was among them—took the opportunity to say a great deal about what they thought of the topic. Mrs Grey gave a mark out of ten. Molly had only done it once before, and received a pretty good mark, but today her hands felt damp as she reached the whiteboard and turned to face the class.

"So," said Mrs Grey, "tell us your thoughts about Moolooran."

Twenty-five pairs of eyes looked back at her. Many frowned, as if daring Molly to say anything bad about the place. A few stared out the window and didn't pay any attention.

Molly coughed. "Well," she said, "Um…"

A chuckle from the front row, met with a frown from Mrs

72

Grey. For all her other faults, the teacher believed in letting people have a fair chance.

"It's a nice town," she continued at last. "The people are friendly and…" Not everyone, of course, but she could hardly say that. "I think the park has a very nice water feature and…"

Silence. A thought awoke in the back of Molly's mind. A memory of her trip to the Council building the day before. She saw Sarika in the third row. Their eyes met, and a small smile broke out on Sarika's face. She gave a slight, almost imperceptible, nod.

Molly cleared her throat again and the tightness in her stomach eased. A warmth came rushing up through her body as she opened her mouth and said, "But I don't like what they're doing to Hallow's Choice."

A little gasp from Mrs Grey. More frowns from the students. Perhaps only a few of them had even heard of the forest at the back of the farm. Or if they had, they didn't know what its name was. Sarika smiled wider.

"They're going to cut it down!" Molly declared. "They're going to turn it into houses. The animals will lose their homes and my mother will lose her farm."

That made more of an impression. The students who had been staring out of the window were listening now.

"It's not fair that the Council can take my mother's farm just because they want to—and other people's houses, too."

Mrs Grey tapped the page in her book. "Yes, Molly," she said quietly, "but your mother will be paid for her farm."

"Not much!" Molly felt hot now. "Not what it's worth. And besides, she doesn't *want* to lose it. My family has been living there a long time. My grandfather owned it, and when he died he left it to my mother. How can the Council be so mean? They sent my mother a letter and told her they were taking the farm and that's that."

Mrs Grey looked at her watch. "That's your two minutes, Molly. Thank you for your speech." She made a mark on a piece of paper and gave it to Molly as she returned to her seat.

Seven out of ten.

"Hallow's Choice," explained Mrs Grey, "is a small forest on the east side of town. Some of you may have seen it while travelling towards Tyson's Creek." She went to a map of the district mounted on the wall. "You can see that Hallow's Choice is here, near the highway. Now the highway is very important to Moolooran, and many more people want to come and live here. So the Council is planning a large housing development here." Mrs Grey pointed at the map. "It'll be great for Moolooran. And I believe Ava's uncle will be building the houses!" All eyes turned on Ava, who smiled at the sudden gift of attention.

"But it's not fair!" Molly clamped her hand over her mouth as soon as the words escaped. The heads of the students turned from Ava to Molly as if watching the ball at a tennis match.

"Of course," said Mrs Grey, "there might be some minor disturbance, and some people might be inconvenienced. But we must consider the community as a whole. Now, for homework I want you all to write a paragraph about what Moolooran means to you."

Groans from some students, who no doubt blamed Molly for the extra homework.

***

"I have a plan," said Molly as she sat next to Sarika on the bus going home. She kept her voice down because the bus was packed with other students, and Ava sat only a few seats away.

Sarika's eyes lit up in a way Molly liked. Unlike just about everyone else at school, Sarika never judged Molly and trusted her to say what was on her mind without prompting.

"I'm going to stage a protest," Molly continued. "I've seen them on TV. You stand outside and hold up a sign and chant slogans and tell people what you want. Or in our case, what we *don't* want."

"Me too?"

Molly had used the words "our" and "we" without thinking.

But of course, Sarika could join her protest. On TV there were always lots of people holding up signs and marching.

"Yes, of course."

"All right," said Sarika. But then her face fell. "But Mama and Papa won't let me go to the forest by myself."

Molly thought for a moment. "Well, maybe they'd like to come also. Or at least keep an eye on you. I'm going to ask Mum if she wants to be in the protest too."

That thought hadn't occurred to Molly until just then. All sorts of surprising and unexpected comments were emerging from her mouth today. Her brain worked hard. "We can get her to give us a lift to that new road that enters the forest. Then, when that dreadful Mr Fanshawe drives past, he'll see us. We can make signs and think of some slogans to chant. They have to be short and easy to remember, you know. I'm no good at words so you could do that."

"And you can make the signs," put in Sarika, wriggling with excitement. "You draw so well."

For the first time in ages, Molly felt good about the future.

***

It took a bit more organising than Molly had anticipated. Mum was a little hesitant at first about Molly's idea for a protest. "We'd look pretty silly just us standing there. Those protest marches with hundreds of people you've seen on TV don't happen overnight."

But when she saw the letter from the Council still lying on the dining room table, she went silent. Soon after Mum's phone rang and she spoke for a long time out on the porch where Molly couldn't hear. After the call she came back in and said, "That was Sarika's father, Dr Jindal. He's keen to participate in a rally if I am." She gave Molly a twisted smile. "You two have this all worked out, haven't you?"

"Not quite all," said Molly. There seemed so much to do now. Never mind Mrs Grey's homework about Moolooran—

Molly had to design posters.

"I'll make a social media page!" Mum announced. "We can find out just how many people might like to protest with us."

So they were all very busy. Mum, now fired up, didn't want to waste time and planned to go out the next day, Friday, to do the protest. "After school, of course," she added when Molly's face lit up the prospect of missing school for a day. "And we'll do it in front of the Town Council building, so everyone can see."

Molly thought that a better idea than at the forest road where she had initially thought.

At school she couldn't focus on her lessons, with her head full of the afternoon's plans. Sarika seemed just as distracted, and both of them were spoken to several times by Mrs Grey. At lunch time they went to the school library and looked at the social media page Mum had made.

"There's only seven people joined up," said Sarika, her mouth twisted in disappointment. "And two of them are my parents, and one is your Mama."

"It's not much of a start," Molly admitted.

"But it *is* a start," said Sarika. "The page has only been up since this morning. You'll see." But her voice didn't sound too confident.

When the final bell eventually rang Mum was waiting for them outside the school gates with Sarika's parents. Mrs Jindal was again dressed in her bright colours; Dr Jindal wore a neat business suit and shook both Molly and her mother's hands. "I am very glad to meet you both," he said in a rich, deep voice. Molly liked him immediately.

The plan, Dr Jindal explained, was to drive into town and park in Dr Jindal's surgery carpark, which was just a short distance from the Council building. From there they would walk to the front steps and ask to speak to the Mayor about the situation. "He won't want to speak to us, of course," Dr Jindal said, "but we will make our point."

"It's just a start," said Mrs Jindal.

When they arrived at the carpark Molly showed them the protest signs she had made and everyone complimented her. One had a picture of a possum in a tree. Over the possum's head were the words, "Please don't take my home away." The other was a map of Hallow's Choice with a large arrow pointing to it. At the other end of the arrow were the words "No houses here!" in bright red paint. Molly had stayed up late to finish them and not once had Mum told her to go to bed.

Dr Jindal and Mum led the way to the Council offices. Mrs Jindal walked behind her husband, the children behind her and several other people who had turned up brought up the rear. It wasn't a formal march and they kept the signs lowered until they reached the Council steps. Molly was about to say how excited she was when something grabbed the back of her leg.

She looked down and saw nothing. But she felt the unmistakable clutch of tiny hands. Invisible hands. A voice said, "What are you doing?"

Obidee!

Molly shook her leg to try to dislodge him. When Mum glanced at her she pretended to scratch it.

"What's the matter?" whispered Sarika.

The sprite's claws continued to clutch at Molly's leg and she continued to shake it. "It's *him!*" she replied, still walking along with invisible Obidee hanging from her leg. "Get off!"

"You mean—the *sprite?*" Sarika's eyes grew wide as she peered at Molly's leg.

"Yes. I…"

"What on earth is the matter with you?' Mum asked. "Hurry up, you two. We must stick together."

They hurried after the others, Molly limping as she raised and lowered her leg, which Obidee rode. She could feel his hard claws clutching at her leg, hoping he didn't leave scratches. His broom-like hair brushed her thigh.

At last they reached the Council steps and Obidee let go. In the bright afternoon sunlight he was quite invisible.

"This is where we make our stand," announced Dr Jindal.

"Right—you two girls, in front there at the bottom step. We grown-ups will stand here near the top."

They took their positions. At this hour many people were on the street, hurrying along on their own business, but as soon as the placards were held up they began to take notice of the small group standing on the steps. Molly felt a little self-conscious clutching her placard. Despite trying to look impressive, she felt just the opposite: small and insignificant.

A few people walked up and down the steps as they entered and left the building. A man in a suit stopped and asked the grown-ups what was going on.

"We are protesting the development of Hallow's Choice," said Dr Jindal sternly.

The man scowled. "What do you mean?"

Dr Jindal indicated the placards as if the man hadn't seen them. "We mean, leave Hallow's Choice alone."

That was one of the slogans Sarika had composed. She and Molly now took up the cry, and roared out, "Leave Hallow's Choice alone!"

"Save the animals!" shrieked Sarika.

"Get out of the forest or I'll smash you!" yelled a harsh voice.

Everyone went quiet.

"Who said that?" asked Mum.

No one replied. Molly hung her head, but it was really so she could try and catch a glimpse of Obidee at her feet and give him a kick. But the bright sun still made him totally invisible.

The man in the suit hurried on his way.

"We're not here to threaten people," said Dr Jindal, glaring at the girls. "That was a very bad thing to say."

"But we didn't, Papa," squeaked Sarika.

Molly clutched her placard and hoped Obidee said nothing more.

They stood there as people went by. Some stayed and asked questions, and Mrs Jindal handed out brochures they had prepared. Some people took the brochures, others refused.

Things were going all right, and Obidee's threat had been forgotten, when a police car pulled up right in front of the Town Hall and two officers emerged. The male officer stayed near the car; the female officer approached and said, "Who is your representative?"

"I am," said Dr Jindal.

"Do you have a permit to hold a rally?" the officer asked. She had sweat on her face, small beads of moisture that made Molly think the woman had already had a long day.

"A permit?" Dr Jindal grinned. "We have a right to protest. It's called freedom of speech."

"That's true," said the officer. "But you also need a permit for a rally of more than three people. Do you have one?"

Anxious looks among the grown-ups. "No," said Dr Jindal.

Mrs Jindal thrust a brochure at the police officer. "You can read about what they are going to do to Hallow's Choice in here."

The officer took the brochure and flicked it open. "I see. Well, I'm sorry, but I have to ask you to move on. You are obstructing the entrance to this building and you don't have a permit."

"Go away!" shouted Obidee, still at Molly's feet.

The officer glanced down at Molly. "Did you say something?"

Molly opened her mouth to say no, but Obidee cried out: "Go away you big bully!"

To her credit, the officer looked around to see if anyone but Molly had spoken. She said to Dr Jindal, "For the second time I'm asking you to move on. If you refuse, I must arrest you for obstruction and refusing the lawful direction of a police officer."

A dark blue vest covered the woman's police uniform and in the pockets were notebooks and pens and a flashlight. On her hip was what Molly first thought was a gun, but it was actually a taser. A compulsion to obey the woman rose, but Molly gripped her placard and didn't move. Neither did anyone else.

"I'm going to ask one final time," said the officer. "As you don't have a permit for this protest, you are in violation of..."

"All right," said Dr Jindal. "We will go. Come along."

The police officer suddenly became polite again. "Thank you," she said. Then she glared down at Molly. "Be careful how you talk to police officers in future, miss. Learn from this gentleman."

Molly was unable to speak as they walked back to the cars. Obidee had told the officer to go away, and yet everyone thought it was her. She almost threw the placard away as they reached the cars, hoping it would hit the sprite.

Sarika grabbed her hand as they rode in the back seat. "It's all right," she whispered. "I know it wasn't you."

"It was..."

"Yes. And I'm very angry with him."

But even Sarika's faith in her innocence didn't help. It was long, silent ride back to the farm.

CHAPTER 11

NATURE'S WAY

The barbed wire fence cut across the sunset as Molly and Sarika stood at the place where the ground dipped a little. Neither had dared slide under the wire. First of all, they had both been expressly forbidden to go into Hallow's Choice. Second, although neither admitted it, they were a little scared.

Obidee had seemed a quaint sort of mysterious friend when Molly first met him. The thrill of knowing a creature that everyone else thought was mere folklore had made her feel special. She had hoped they might go on being friends. But things had changed with his attempt to kill Ava and making her sound disrespectful at the protest several days ago. She needed to speak with him, and this seemed the only opportunity.

Dr Jindal had spent the days since the protest applying for a permit to hold a formal rally. There seemed a lot of forms to fill in and Dr Jindal had to go for an interview and they had to form a proper group with a name and have it registered or something; Molly couldn't follow all the grown-up stuff. Adult things worked far too slowly for her.

All of them—the Jindals, Mum and the children—had gathered for a meeting, and Mum had noticed Molly fidgeting and not really paying attention. She suggested the girls go and play while the adults discussed things. Molly had hurried Sarika outside and towards the fence.

No sign of Obidee, of course.

"Typical," said Molly as they stood staring into the forest. "When I *didn't* want to see him, he clung to my leg. Now when I *do*, he isn't around."

"I want to see him," said Sarika. "I've never seen a sprite. Well, not properly. Just that glimpse in the classroom."

"For a wood sprite, he seems to spend a lot of time out of the wood."

"We can't just stand here," said Sarika. "Someone will notice and ask what we're doing."

It would help, thought Molly grimly, if they actually did know what they were doing. "Obidee!" she called softly, but knew her voice at that level had no hope of reaching even the closest trees. "Nothing for it," she said, "we have to go in."

Sarika glanced over her shoulder. "My father would not let me."

"He won't find out."

The breeze that stirred her nut-brown hair felt oddly chilly, and the forest almost as scary as it did the first night she'd gone in. But the urge to enter, as if the trees beckoned her on, had returned.

"Are you all right?" asked Sarika.

Molly found herself holding the top strand of barbed wire. The barbs dug into her flesh. She unclasped her hand and stared at the dents made in her palm.

"Yes," she said.

"You looked...I don't know." Sarika stroked Molly's hand with her finger. "Are you cut?"

"No." She went to where the ground allowed them to slide under the wire. "I'm going in. Are you coming?"

Another look over her shoulder and Sarika nodded, but her eyes still showed a trace of anxiety.

Molly scrambled under the barbed wire and made sure it didn't catch on her coat this time. Sarika, smaller and with a less bulky jacket, made it through more easily. They scurried into the trees and came to the dense undergrowth. "It gets tricky from here," Molly said, leading the way.

She recognised nothing from her previous trips under the trees. Each occasion had been at a different time of day, and the light made all the difference. With full daylight the trees seemed further apart, the undergrowth less thick, and the colours made it easier to distinguish distance and forms. At night, on Molly's first entrance, all had been spooky and black. Now, in the evening, the orange light from the setting sun cast long shadows that made things a little confusing, but not too much. A heavy silence lay over everything, and that gave a tone of expectancy, almost as if time had halted, waiting for something.

You asked me to come in, she thought. *You, the forest, wanted me here.* She waited for a response, but now they were under the trees, the strange compulsion to be there had faded.

She jumped at the sudden whistle of a butcherbird.

"I think we're in deep enough here," she said. "I'm going to give a call." She put both hands up to her mouth. "Obidee!"

The word fell flat among the trees. She tried again, "Obidee!"

Something moved in the undergrowth. Sarika squealed as a long grey lizard broke cover at her feet and hurried off between the trees.

"I'm sorry," she said to Molly. "I'm just really nervous being here. If my parents find out…"

Molly nodded. "Yes. This is hopeless. Obidee could be anywhere in the forest—or not even here at all." Her desire to see the sprite had also faded. Why had she wanted to, anyway? To tell him off for pushing Ava under a car? For being rude to the police officer? He wouldn't listen.

"Come on," she said, following the words with a heavy sigh. "Let's go home."

Sarika pointed. "Wait! What's that?"

The sun had set more now, the long shadows thrown by the trees blending together into a general twilight. In a few minutes it would be quite dark, and they would be expected back at the farm and indoors.

But something moved in the shadows, a small figure that separated from the undergrowth and took a few steps towards the girls. Still a little transparent, but becoming more solid as the light faded, Obidee appeared before them.

"Hello," he said, his voice a little uncertain. "Did you want to see me?"

"My goodness!" said Sarika, stepping back to put Molly between her and the sprite. "He's real."

Obidee folded his skinny twig-thin arms across his stick-like chest and snarled, "Of course I am. As real as you."

Molly gripped Sarika's hand to reassure her. She wanted to say that Obidee wouldn't hurt her, but now she wasn't so sure. "Hello, Obidee," she said. "Yes, I wanted to speak with you. You've been doing bad things."

"Yes. Have you come here to thank me?" A cheeky smile broke out on the sprite's face, like a crack in tree bark.

"*Thank* you?" Molly snarled so loudly the sprite retreated behind a small bush. His smile vanished as quickly as it came. "Thank you for what? For almost killing Ava? For dropping a drawer on Mrs Grey's foot? For almost getting me arrested? Why should I thank you for any of that?"

The sprite did his little dance and pointed a long finger at the girls. "I was trying to help you. That girl was mean to you—to both of you. And I thought you wanted to be rude to people. That's what your protest was all about."

"You've been following me. Keeping invisible in the daylight and following me everywhere. Listening in. How dare you."

The sprite's forehead narrowed and his hair bristled even more upright than usual. "I'm a *sprite*, Molly. I'm a forest creature. That's the way we live here, keeping our eyes and ears open, hiding, following without being heard. That's what we do to survive."

As if on cue, the lizard that had startled them before emerged from its hiding place in some long grass and slunk towards a tree. It stared up at the trunk for a moment, then darted upwards, catching an insect that Molly hadn't noticed until that moment. It swallowed the bug and vanished again into the wood.

"There!" declared Obidee. "That's nature's way. Hide and hunt and you stay alive. I've been hiding and hunting."

"But other people get hurt," said Sarika quietly. "Why did you push Ava in front of that car?"

"I didn't!"

"Yes, you did!" cried Molly, but realised in that moment that of course she hadn't actually seen Obidee push the girl, since he was invisible. It's just that Ava fell forwards in a really strange way.

But her insistence had an effect on Obidee. He stamped his foot and held his hands to his head. "All right, I did. But as I said, that's the way nature does things. The strong survive."

"The *strong?*" Sarika shrieked. "You weren't strong pushing Ava in front of that car. You were a bully, just like her."

"I was teaching her a lesson."

"By trying to kill her?" Molly let go of Sarika's hand and shook her fist at Obidee. "How does she learn a lesson if she's dead?"

"I didn't want to kill her. Just scare her."

Molly thought that was a very dangerous way to do it. "I'd *like* to help save the forest—" she said.

"We both would," put in Sarika.

"But in the way that *people* do it. That protest was one of the ways. We weren't there to be a nuisance to people, or scare or insult them. Just to tell them what we think."

A little laugh from Obidee. A sour, short laugh that carried no humour whatsoever. "Well you didn't do a very good job."

He had a point, but Molly didn't dare say so.

"We're doing more," put in Sarika, who didn't hang onto Molly anymore. "My Papa is planning a big protest and this time we won't be in trouble from the police. There'll be hundreds of people, you'll see. My Papa is very good at organising things."

"By that time," Obidee replied, "the forest will be cut down and I won't have a home. And nor will your mother!"

Molly decided at that moment that Obidee was just as bad a bully as Ava, just as mean as Mr Fanshawe, and just as grown-up as Mrs Grey. She clenched her fists and her words came from a tight mouth.

"That's not true! We have to work together, don't you see?"

"Then work with me. With us. We'll wreck the cars, scare the people cutting down the forest."

"No! That's bad."

"But bad works!"

Silence for a moment. Molly became aware of movement in the bushes and among the trees. A bird fluttered its wings in branches over her head. The lizard, perched on a log with its hood raised, slowly moved its tail. Two eyes of a sleepy possum stared out at her from another tree. The air was suddenly full of midges and flies that had come from nowhere, crawling on her face and into her eyes. She resisted the urge to slap them.

"It works for nature," she said. "Not for people."

"Then people are only good at ruining everything," said Obidee quietly.

Molly had the nasty feeling he was right. "Come on, Sarika," she said. "We'd better get back."

They turned and started home without another word, or even a goodbye to Obidee. Just as they stepped under a large wattle tree the sprite's voice came to them.

"I'll see you again. The forest wants you."

"What do you mean?" Molly asked.

"I know the trees and animals call to you," he said. "That's what makes you come here. You can't help it. You and the forest need each other."

"Come *on*," urged Sarika, pulling at Molly's hand. "We have to go."

They walked back to the farm slowly. Molly felt the urge to be in the forest rise again. So it called to her, *wanted* her to stay. Obidee was right—she would be back. There was no choice. She looked over her shoulder but could see no sign of the sprite.

***

"Where have you two been?" Dr Jindal loomed large in

Mum's living room and glared at them.

"I'm sorry, Papa," said Sarika. "Molly was showing me the farm."

Behind Dr Jindal, Mrs Jindal and Mum looked at each other. There were coffee cups on the dining room table along with many papers and books. In a corner, curled up but also looking accusingly at the girls, lay Tessa.

"As long as you didn't go into the forest," said Dr Jindal. "Because I looked out the back door for you and I couldn't see you."

"I asked Tessa to see if she could find you," added her mother. "She had a sniff around the yard but came back alone."

"Yes," said Molly. "I'm sorry, we…" She was about to admit they had trespassed into Hallow's Choice against all orders not to, but she still burned with anger from their argument with Obidee. She said, a little too quickly, "We were down near Mr Drummond's fence. We saw Tessa but she didn't come any closer."

A lie. Molly felt choked, but she couldn't admit the truth. Adults didn't believe in things like sprites. It was most unfair that the truth would only be taken for a lie.

After a short silence Dr Jindal glanced at Mum, who nodded. "All right," he said. "We will accept your apologies. But don't wander off again, Sarika. You know your mother worries."

"Yes, Papa. I'm sorry, Mama."

"Take Sarika to your room, Molly," said Mum. "We'll be a little while longer here."

The girls fell onto Molly's bed together.

"You lied," said Sarika. "I lied too, because I didn't say anything."

"But we couldn't tell the truth." Molly stared up at the plastic stars on the ceiling. Exploring hostile alien landscapes would be much preferable to lying to her mother.

"Lying is what Obidee would do," said Sarika.

.

CHAPTER 12

MOLLY GOES LIVE

Molly soon changed her mind about Dr Jindal's organisation of the protest group. He made everyone feel confident and enthusiastic about the big event he and Mum planned for the following week. Trucks and roadwork vehicles had already assembled at the road leading into Hallow's Choice, ready to cut down the forest, and Dr Jindal intended that a public protest rally be staged in town before they removed a single tree.

Another good thing was that Mr Fanshawe left Molly's mother alone now, not coming to the farm to demand she sell it to his company. Of course, the court hearing still loomed where Mum intended to object to the acquisition of the property, but that was a long way ahead. Dr Jindal had arranged for a friend in town who was a lawyer to help, and as a favour he was charging Mum a lot less money than he normally might.

So when her mother called Molly to her one day, Molly was pleased to see a smile on her face.

"You're going to be famous," her mother said.

Molly's heart gave a little skip. "How?"

"The local radio station has asked to interview you. Our little protest at the Town Hall last week didn't go unnoticed. And particularly your comments to the police officer."

"But I..." Molly started to protest then decided to keep quiet, especially as her mother raised a finger to shush her.

"We won't go into that again. *But*—the local radio station has a talk show on each week. It's a program where people can ring in and discuss issues of interest. And they want you to be their guest for Monday's show! They want to interview the girl who stood her ground against the Council."

"But…" Molly thought herself so uninteresting. She just sat there for a moment.

"Well, Molly, what do you think? You don't have to do it if you don't want to."

Molly thought hard. It would be good to go on the air and discuss the proposal to cut down Hallow's Choice. More people would hear about it that way, and might decide to join the protest. On the other hand, she could imagine Ava and her cronies teasing her about being on the air, and what if she froze completely and couldn't say anything? She recalled her terrible performance in front of the class at Impromptu Speaking.

"I don't know," she said quietly.

"Now, Molly, I'm sure Dr Jindal would be delighted if you went on the radio. You could mention the planned protest. They've already said that's one thing they want to talk about."

Molly had never done anything like this in her life. She thought about sitting there in a room with the radio announcer, answering questions and talking about herself. A little thrill went through her—it would be fun, perhaps.

"Will you come with me?" she asked.

"Of course. They want an adult to be present."

Molly's reply took ages coming up right from her stomach and along her throat and eventually emerging out of her mouth. "All right," she said.

***

The radio station was smaller than Molly had imagined. It was no bigger than the local library, and that was small enough. She had thought anything as important as a radio station had to be enormous. Where was the towering transmitter and the hundreds of people who must work there? None of that existed.

The smiling young man who met her and her mother at the front desk wore an open-necked shirt and black jeans and had a mop of long black hair. His name was Terry Ballard and he shook Molly's hand in a different way to how Dr Jindal had done. Terry's grip was looser, less formal. She liked him, but again not in the same way as Dr Jindal. Molly never realised shaking hands could be such an informative experience.

"So, you're the girl who told off the cops," Terry said, but smiled at the same time.

"Is that how you're going to announce her?" asked Mum.

"What? No, of course not. Just saying…" He paused under Mum's stare—a stare Molly knew only too well.

They went through to a small office. Terry's desk was the messiest Molly had ever seen. Even the chairs were covered in papers and bits of electronic equipment, so they couldn't sit down.

"There's another show on at the moment, playing in Studio 2, one of the agricultural ones." He turned up a speaker on the wall and the voice of an announcer came through, talking about crop prices. "We'll go through to Studio 1 now and I'll introduce you to Cathy."

Molly was surprised to see the studio was little more than a tiny room with a glass panel at one end, a desk and several chairs. Three microphones came out of the centre of the desk, and the biggest one loomed over a bank of complicated-looking controls. Behind a glass partition sat a middle-aged woman. On seeing them, she opened a connecting door and Molly once again experienced shaking hands. Cathy's grip felt important, but less friendly.

"Cathy is the engineer," explained Terry. "She'll make sure people can hear us, and will line up the people who phone in."

"Will there be many of those?" asked Molly.

Terry laughed. "Well, we don't know until they ring, but I'm sure what you have to say will be interesting."

"How many people do you think will be listening in?" asked her mother. Molly wished she hadn't—the thought of lots of listeners made her nervous.

"Our weekly average is about a thousand," replied Terry.

That didn't make Molly feel any better. An image went through her mind of whole rows and ranks of people sitting listening to her words, leaning towards their radios, or putting earbuds in to hear her words while riding on the bus. "We're an FM station—that means our broadcast goes out in stereo."

"Yes, I know," said Molly, proud to know something at last. "And AM means it doesn't. We learned about it in Science."

"Of course you did." Terry smiled and sat down in the chair in front of the big microphone. In a few minutes he had both Molly and her mother sitting opposite him. Cathy adjusted Molly's microphone and then had her put on a pair of earphones. They felt heavy and she hoped she didn't have to wear them long. When Terry spoke, she heard him through the earphones.

"When Cathy gives us the signal," he said, "I'll introduce the show and you. It's really important you don't make a sound until I say hello to you. Okay?"

Molly nodded, the excitement rising in her. The clock's minute hand moved slowly towards the hour, and before she knew it there came a blast of music through her headphones and Terry began talking in a smooth, rounded voice quite unlike his ordinary one.

"Hello out there, and welcome to 'What's New?'. I'm Terry Ballard and today we'll be discussing the proposal by the Moolooran Council to go ahead with the Hallow's Choice development. This development's been on the books for a while and, if it goes ahead, all of Hallow's Choice will be cut down and turned into houses. We know that some people welcome this as a boon for the town, and others condemn it. So, today's question is: what is the price of progress? We look forward to your views. With me today to give her own perspective is someone we'd all like on our side, I'm sure." He gave Molly a quick wink. "Molly Travers, an eleven-year-old student at Moolooran State School, made a bit of a stir last week when she stood outside the Town Hall and waved a placard begging them not to cut down Hallow's Choice. Hello, Molly."

Her cue. She glanced at Mum, who nodded, gulped so loudly she wondered if the microphone picked it up, and said, "Hello, Terry."

"So, Molly, I understand you're against the development. Why is that?"

Molly bit her lip. This wasn't like Impromptu Speaking in Mrs Grey's class at all. No rows of students looking back at her; no teacher lurking nearby with a pencil ready to rate her performance. Just a huge, silver microphone and a smiling Terry, who had the good sense not to look at her. She gripped her right hand in a tight fist and said, "Because it's not fair! They want to take my mother's house away from her, and other people's houses too. They've worked a long time to make those places into homes. And the animals of the forest—what will happen to them? Are there any plans to put them in some other place? Everything has a right to a life, and the Hallow's Choice people want to take those lives away."

Terry nodded. "And so when you stood outside the Town Hall the other day, you were making a stand on behalf of the homeowners and people?"

"Yes."

"You had a bit of a run in with a police officer, didn't you?"

Molly gaped. She hadn't expected such a direct question. She glanced at Mum, who also looked a bit put out. Molly became aware of the heavy silence.

"I never did!" she declared. "People keep telling me I was rude to a policewoman, but I never was. That was someone else."

"Someone else in your little protest group?"

"No. Someone…I don't know."

She sank back in her chair. How unfair!

Fortunately, Terry held up his hand. "And we have our first caller already. Yes, caller, you're on the air."

For the next ten minutes Molly said very little. Several people called in and made comments. A couple were for the development, and gave reasons why. Another caller, an elderly man, said he thought Molly was a brave girl who was doing the right thing. That made her feel better. He asked her a direct question. "Molly, how can I help out? Is there some way I can support your protest group?"

"You can go to our social media page and sign up," she replied promptly. She gave the page's address—fortunately she'd written it down on a slip of paper so she wouldn't forget. "We want everyone to turn up to our rally next week and show the Council we mean business!"

This got smiles from both Terry and Mum, and the caller said, "That's the spirit, Molly. Good for you! I'll sign up right away."

About five minutes later there came another call. Terry said, "Hello, caller. And what do you have to say about all this?"

The voice that came through Molly's headphones sent a shiver down her spine.

"I'm Jacob Fanshawe," the voice said. "I'm the CEO and chairman of the company carrying out this development."

Even Terry seemed impressed. "Well, hello, Mr Fanshawe, welcome to the show. And what would you like to say?"

"Well first up, I have to say that the Hallow's Choice development is a great leap ahead for the district. More people are coming to the shire every year, and most are going to settle right here in town. As a progressive company, we want to ensure that they and their families have a decent place to live. Secondly, I think your little protester there has it wrong. We aren't going to just cut down the forest and build houses. Hallow's Choice will be a well-planned residential centre with parks, gardens, play areas and landscaped zones where both people and animals will be able to live."

"But you want my mother's farm!" piped in Molly. "You want to take away from my family the place we've had for so long."

There was silence for one second, then Mr Fanshawe's calm voice came back, "You sound like a smart young lady, but I don't think that you fully understand this development. It's for everyone's good, and sometimes changes are necessary."

"But the animals!"

"A few snakes and lots of ants? I don't think anyone will miss those."

"But there's other animals too! Possums and wallabies and lizards. I've seen them. And there's…oh!"

She'd almost said there was a wood sprite living there, but stopped herself just in time.

"There's other animals too."

"And there are a lot of people wanting Moolooran to be the number one town in the district," said the calm, slow voice of Mr Fanshawe. "What's more important: people and progress, or a strip of tangled forest no one even visits anymore?"

Terry spoke up, "Well, thanks for your views, Mr Fanshawe. I'm sure that if anyone wants more information, they can go to your company."

"That's right, Terry," replied Mr Fanshawe. "It's always a good idea to check out the facts first before you venture an opinion."

He hung up.

Molly sat back in her chair, feeling very warm despite the air conditioning. Her mother reached out and touched her shoulder gently.

CHAPTER 13

THE DESTRUCTION SITE

By the first day of the school holidays, Molly was exhausted.

There had been so much to do in the last week, and not a lot of time to do it in. Not only had she had to keep up with her schoolwork, but also prepare lots of placards for the upcoming rally.

Everyone else had been busy too. Having obtained a permit for the protest, Dr Jindal organised a lot of other people to assemble at the Anzac memorial in the town centre. From there, they would march on Town Hall—with the help of the police this time—and holding their placards. At the Town Hall, Dr Jindal and Mum, as representatives of the assembly, would present the mayor with a formal letter of protest, signed by a lot of people, about the Hallow's Choice development.

Mrs Jindal had taken charge of several other women to run a stall, also with permission, selling cakes and other baked goods to raise money for the protest and for further action against the development.

Mum had composed a special fanfare on her trumpet, which she would play as they marched. Even Molly had to admit it sounded impressive, if a little short.

The rally was arranged for the first day of holidays so that other children could participate. But there had been just as much divided opinion among the students as there had among the adults. Ava, of course, had thought the whole idea of a protest silly, but then Molly hadn't asked for her opinion, so that didn't count. But a small group of students had promised to turn up. For some reason, the teachers remained silent on the topic. On the morning of the rally, however, Molly noticed several teachers in the group that assembled, and almost all of the students who had promised.

"A good turnout," said Dr Jindal, once again clad in his dark, formal suit and tie.

"I was hoping for more," put in Mum, but Dr Jindal never dropped his wide smile. He had just finished helping Mrs Jindal and other ladies set up their stall, which was already doing a brisk trade.

Sarika tapped Molly's arm and pointed. "Look! The newspaper is here."

A van pulled up with the name *Moolooran Times* on it. Several people got out and one started taking pictures. In a minute Dr Jindal was talking to another reporter, and Molly could see why he wore the suit on a warm day, because it made him look most dignified.

"I wonder if we'll get our pictures in the paper?' asked Sarika. Molly knew her friend was jealous of her radio appearance a week ago.

"If we stand behind your dad we might."

But Dr Jindal was more interested in marching than talking. After a few minutes with the reporter, he addressed the assembled crowd through a portable loudspeaker he had ordered in from the city. "Everyone! Can you hear me, please? We are about to march on Town Hall, so form an orderly line. Families together, others where you will. Hold your placards and banners high!"

It took a little while for people to sort themselves out. Some women pushed prams. Some young children had dressed up as animals so there was a kangaroo and a koala and a wombat marching along with the humans. Molly had her old banner from the first protest. Sarika had a new one she had made herself. It said simply, "Hands off our homes."

Molly wore a wide-brimmed hat around which she had entwined some gum leaves and wattle, both trees found in

Hallow's Choice. She glanced around in case Obidee had shown up, but of course in the bright sunlight the sprite would be invisible. For days now Molly had been checking behind her, listening to noises in the night, scared that the sprite might be hiding somewhere, or tracking her. But there had been no sign of him.

A blast from Mum's trumpet drew her attention back to the rally. They were off. Dr Jindal had put himself and Mum at the front and the children walked immediately behind them, Molly and Sarika holding their placards. Mum blared on her trumpet all the way.

Many people of the town who had not elected to march were watching from the footpaths. A couple of police officers were there too, including the female officer who had stopped the last rally. Now she walked along beside them, keeping an eye on things.

There were some people in the watching crowd, Molly noticed, who held other signs. One read, "Develop the Forest". Another, "We need houses." But on the whole these people were few in number. Most people cheered and waved as they walked by.

Molly felt really important, like she was actually doing something positive about stopping Mr Fanshawe's plans. She held her head up and strode along, the wattle on her hat bobbing with each step.

But still she kept an eye out for Obidee.

They halted on the footpath outside the Town Hall. Quite a crowd had assembled there, too, and waited to see the fun. The newspaper van arrived, and a crew with a television camera was already waiting to report on the proceedings.

"Being on TV would be even better than radio," Molly said to Sarika, who nodded.

Her mother blew yet another fanfare on her trumpet, but must have been nervous with the television camera pointing at her and she flubbed a couple of notes. Dr Jindal stepped forward as a reporter came up with a microphone.

"This is an important petition for the Mayor," he declared, "and I formally call upon His Worship to come out and receive it."

As if on cue, the doors of the Town Hall opened, but it was only an old lady with a basket of shopping. She halted at the top of the steps, staring at all the people.

"Oh dear," she muttered, and walked slowly down and on her way. A small chuckle went through the crowd.

Then the doors opened again and the Mayor came out, flanked by two other people: a woman who wore a pair of thin-framed spectacles, and Mr Fanshawe himself. The Mayor was making no pretence about being impartial.

"I receive this petition from Dr Jindal," said the Mayor straight to the television camera, "and I thank him and all the concerned citizens of Moolooran here today."

"Give us a fair go!" someone in the crowd called. For a second Molly thought it was Obidee: the voice was almost exactly like his. But it was just a young man in the crowd.

"Everyone will receive a fair go, I assure you," smiled the Mayor. "Things are already in place out at the construction site, and I can assure you all that the work will cause as little disruption as possible." He stepped closer to the microphone and uttered more about how important the development was to the town. All the time, Mr Fanshawe glared at Molly, and she glared back at him, clutching her placard.

While the Mayor was answering questions, a police officer stepped up to Mr Fanshawe and spoke some words Molly couldn't hear. Mr Fanshawe's mouth twisted down and his eyebrows almost came together. Molly saw him mouth the word, "What?" to the officer.

A moment later the two of them stepped away from the Mayor, who was still in full flight. They spoke together very earnestly for a minute. Then the officer beckoned Dr Jindal, who joined them. He went through exactly the same process, frowning and mouthing "What?" Then she shook his head very hard and said something else.

Molly sidled nearer, while still facing the Mayor. As she came closer, she heard Mr Fanshawe say, "This is a disgrace."

"It wasn't anyone I know," Dr Jindal said. "I can assure you of that."

"You don't know all these people," replied Mr Fanshawe. "This is just the sort of low act I'd expect."

The police officer put up a hand. "Now, gentlemen, all we can do at this stage is assess the damage. The question of who is responsible will have to come later."

Mr Fanshawe looked about to say something else, but he didn't, and stalked away, pulling out his phone.

"What happened?" Molly asked Dr Jindal.

"Someone has caused damage at the Hallow's Choice construction site," he replied slowly. "And a tree has been placed across the road, barring access. But it couldn't have been anyone here."

Molly didn't need to think who might have done such a thing.

***

"This is dreadful."

Molly had never seen such wanton destruction. The small clearing at the start of the road into Hallow's Choice was filled with vehicles and equipment, and almost all of them had been damaged in some way. A truck had all its tyres blown—not just let down but burst. A bulldozer had somehow been pushed over, lying on its side like a fallen elephant. Broken chainsaws and other tools lay everywhere. Across the road a little way into the forest was a dead tree trunk. The tree had fallen some time ago, maybe years, but it had now been dragged from wherever it had originally lain and blocked the road off. Already men were working with chainsaws to remove the thing, but it would take a while.

Mr Fanshawe stood by the overturned bulldozer talking to the news reporter. Molly stared in disbelief at the fallen machine. It must weigh many tons, and yet it had been tossed over as if it were nothing. Could Obidee have done such a thing?

"This is clearly a case of vandalism on a gross level," Mr Fanshawe said, and the news reporter copied his words down. "I will make sure that whoever did this is found and punished."

"Who do you think could do such a thing?" the reporter asked. "I mean, it would have taken a lot of people, don't you think, to tip over a whole bulldozer."

Mr Fanshawe folded his arms and turned his head as if looking around, although his sunglasses hid his eyes. "There are some people who object to this project," he said. "That is clear from today's protest. I don't want to mention any names at this point."

Molly looked at the dead tree placed across the road entrance. The same strength that had overturned the bulldozer had to be used to pull or push this massive trunk here. To one side of the road was a gouge in the forest floor where the tree had been dragged. The gouge went for at least twenty metres.

She walked along the gouge and stopped where the earth had been torn up. This must be where the tree had originally stood. Bare soil had been scattered over the undergrowth, spreading the disturbed area wider. Several brushes had been knocked over as the tree had been hauled along to its final position.

No sign of anything else. If whoever—whatever—had moved the dead tree left any tracks, they weren't visible. She remembered the small footprint Obidee had left when she had first entered the forest, but there was nothing like that now.

She stared into the undergrowth, walking a few more paces deeper between the trees. No animals, no calling birds, just the silence of the deep bush. Brown dirt and grass, fallen timber, dead leaves. Silence over everything.

Silence! Not even any insects. Normally the woods would be full of buzzing, chirping, the crackle of cicadas, the drone of flies. For the first time ever while in the wood, no insects bothered Molly. The silence worked into her mind, an awful silence that made the whole place seem dead. The sound of the chainsaws had stopped.

Molly put out a hand and touched a stringybark tree beside her. The papery bark felt dryer than normal, but the scrape of her fingers along it made no sound at all. She gouged her fingernails into the bark slightly and dragged down, but nothing came to her ears.

"Molly!"

Her mother's voice broke the spell. Molly ran back along the track of the fallen tree, and immediately became aware of the chainsaws again, not starting up from being turned off, but suddenly coming back in mid-roar.

A shadow passed from the sun.

"There you are," said Mum. "I was worried. Don't go wandering off again." She pointed at the chainsaw gang. "You might get hurt." Just as she said this a large branch fell from the tree and crashed to the ground.

The Jindal family walked up, Sarika between her parents, holding a hand of each. "There is no point staying here," said Dr Jindal. "Whoever did this hasn't helped our side. This isn't a construction site—it's more of a *de*struction site."

"But who could have done it?" asked Mrs Jindal. "That tree—and the bulldozer!"

"Yes, that is odd," agreed Dr Jindal. "But there's nothing we can do."

They walked to their cars, but as the Jindals neared their vehicle Sarika broke away and ran over to Molly.

"You're thinking of something," the girl said.

"Yes," said Molly. "I want to find Obidee and see if he is behind this. I tried to find him just a minute ago and something was strange."

"What?" To her credit, Sarika's eyes were filled with excitement rather than fear.

Molly explained about the silence. "Tonight," she said, "I want to go into the forest and find him. No matter what."

"I want to come too," said Sarika. Then her face fell. "But I live in town, and it's too far."

"Not if you stay the night with me at the farm. Let's go and ask our parents."

There followed a long conversation with Dr and Mrs Jindal and Molly's Mum, but in the end they agreed that Sarika could sleep the night at the farm. Both of Sarika's parents looked a bit tired and perhaps they felt the disappointment of the destruction and what it meant for turning the town against them. They would drop Sarika off at the farm once she had put together an overnight bag.

"So that's settled," said Molly to Sarika when they were alone again. "But we'll have to go after we're supposed to be in bed."

"We'll make it at midnight," said Sarika, her eyes gleaming with the prospect of adventure.

Molly felt most conspiratorial. "We'll take torches and some water," she said. "And dress warmly. And wear decent shoes."

"I will." Sarika hurried back to her parents and Molly opened the door to Mum's car.

As she climbed in, she wondered what the night would hold for them both.

CHAPTER 14

IN THE FORESTS OF THE NIGHT

Molly resisted the urge to turn her torch on to check the batteries. Any light might betray them, especially after the attack on Mr Fanshawe's equipment. He probably had men guarding the site now. The moon was down, but the destruction site would be lit and anyone guarding it wouldn't take kindly to intruders.

She thought about the things in her backpack: a water bottle, some food bars, spare batteries for the torch, her warm jacket and a whistle. She felt like an explorer. Beside her, Tessa sat quietly, tongue lolling out in that doggy way.

Of course, Molly was taking the Irish setter. Although Obidee was afraid of the dog, and might keep him away, Tessa could always find the way home if they got lost, and if it came to it, Molly could use Tessa to protect them. Not that she wanted it to come to that.

A sound came from the old vegetable gardens. A dark shape loomed up—for a moment Molly thought her mother had come looking for her. But Sarika appeared, small and carrying a torch and her own backpack. The darkness had made her seem larger.

"It's me," the girl said unnecessarily as she squatted down beside them.

"Where have you been?" replied Molly. The two girls had shared Molly's bedroom, Sarika sleeping on a spare mattress on the floor until they woke up just before midnight for their expedition. Everything had been packed ready before they went to sleep, but for some reason Sarika had told Molly to go ahead and wait for her by the fence.

"I felt sick." Sarika's eyes were wide. "My tummy plays up if I get nervous and I thought I might…" She broke off and Molly didn't press for any more explanation. She knew what it was like to feel so nervous you think you might throw up.

Molly smiled. "Are you ok now?"

"Yes. I think so."

"Good. We have to find Obidee quickly. We can't be out all night."

They crept along to the low point under the fence. They had to take their backpacks off and push them under the wire before they could follow. Tessa, as usual, had no problem. Sarika got caught on a barb and Molly had to lift the wire up. There was a long gash in Sarika's shirt.

"Mama will wonder where I got that."

They hurried across the forest and stood for a moment looking in.

Molly had been under the trees several times now, both during the day and at night. Each time the forest had been a little different, either friendly or not. This time, without a moon and with the breeze a little cold under the stars, the leaves rattled and rustled more than usual. Darkness lurked under the trees, unrelieved by any rays of moonlight sneaking down. The forest looked blacker than at any other time, and most uninviting.

"Well, come on," she said, and stepped forward. Sarika followed.

About ten metres in, they stopped in a small hollow. Several white stones lay among the grass stems, and a fallen tree thrust a long branch up into the air. Molly tied her handkerchief to the branch. "There, that will show us the way out," she said.

"Now which way?"

Molly turned her torch on and swung it around. Since Obidee could only be seen in darkness, shining a light on him would simply turn him invisible, but she and Sarika needed light to move anywhere. Trying to clamber blindly through the undergrowth would not be easy, even with Tessa.

The most likely place to find Obidee, Molly had reasoned, was either in the small bower he had shown her, or near the destruction site. She wasn't confident about finding the first; she wasn't happy about going near the second. But to get to either they first had to find the road.

"This way," and Molly ploughed on, holding Tessa's lead. Sarika followed behind, making as little noise as possible. They crunched over dead leaves and tripped on rocks, and pushed branches away from their faces. Molly had to be careful not to let a branch swing back and hit Sarika.

"It's so quiet," said Sarika after a few minutes.

Exactly the same as earlier that day when Molly had followed the gouge made by the fallen tree. No insects, no scurrying sounds of animals in the undergrowth. Nothing but their own feet and Tessa's panting. The silence made Molly step as quietly as she could, but that just slowed their progress and made the whole thing more difficult.

"Obidee will hear us a long way off," she said.

They halted under a large gum tree and sipped some water. "This is hard," said Sarika, then added quickly, "but I don't want to go home. It's just a little spooky."

Molly recalled what Sarika had said about ghosts, and wished she hadn't brought them to mind. "I think it's this way," she said, although not feeling that was true at all. "Come on."

Moving was better than staying still. The sound of their feet on the ground, while seemingly loud, was at least better than the oppressive silence that descended if they stood still. After another ten minutes Tessa let out a small growl and stopped walking.

Molly untangled the lead from where it had caught on a small bush, thinking that's what had made the dog stop. But when free, Tessa continued to growl.

"What is it?" Molly asked, but of course the dog didn't reply.

"She's afraid," said Sarika.

Afraid? A big dog like Tessa couldn't be afraid of anything in this forest—but of course, she was an animal, and there were no animals here. And maybe there were no animals for a good reason, and Tessa, being an animal, knew the reason.

All this flashed through Molly's mind as she tugged on the lead trying to move Tessa on. But the dog just sat there and uttered strange noises from deep in her throat.

"I don't like this," said Sarika, shining her torch ahead into the tangled trees ahead. "Maybe we should—"

Another low growl from Tessa, louder, longer. Molly felt the dog tremble as she clutched her fur.

"Turn your torch off!" urged Molly, and blinked in the total darkness that followed. It took a moment for her eyes to adjust, and when they did all that could be seen were the trees and undergrowth. And yet something else skulked out there in the darkness, something that frightened even Tessa.

Molly knelt down beside the dog. She had never feared the dark like this before. The ceiling of stars in her bedroom on the farm comforted her. In the city where she used to live there was always light of some kind. But now, here in the forest, her legs shook and she held her breath. Beside her, Sarika stood rooted in place, hunched a little as she gripped her torch in both hands. The torch wavered a little.

Out in the night, something watched them.

No, it was more than that. Molly became aware of many things: a presence in one place; a slight distortion to the darkness in another; a feeling of something alive, malevolent and totally aware just behind her.

They were surrounded.

The animals had not all gone from the forest. They were still there, but totally silent, all gathered to watch these intrusive humans, tracking them, *hunting* them. Eyes stared at them: the wide eyes of possums, the narrower eyes of wallabies, birds' eyes in the trees and many other eyes, all the more scary because their owners could not be seen.

Molly couldn't stand it anymore.

"Go away!" she barked.

The words fell flat, absorbed by the night.

"That won't do any good," said Sarika in a tiny voice. "They're all around us. It's their forest. Don't you see?"

Yes. She and Sarika were not in charge here. This was untamed forest. Nothing human belonged here.

"Let's go home," said Sarika. "They want us to go home."

But Molly stepped forward, still gripping Tessa's leash like it was a life-line thrown to her in a wild sea, and addressed the unseen animals. "I want to speak to Obidee."

Nothing happened, but the feeling of imminent dread remained. There might have been some movement to her left, but it might just as well have been the wind shifting leaves.

"Please," said Molly. "Where is Obidee? Only-By-Darkness. I want to speak to him."

He could not be here, for in the gloom he would be totally visible. But perhaps the animals knew where he was, or could take a message.

"Is he at the destruction site?" A horrible thought arose that of course these were only animals, and couldn't speak English at all.

Tessa pulled on her leash and out of Molly's grip. The dog stalked away into the forest, not hurrying, but moving almost as quietly as the other animals.

"Come on," said Molly, and the two girls followed Tessa. Occasionally the dog looked behind, as if urging them on. Molly had never felt so helpless, her legs moving as if by themselves, with no will on her part. Even when her long brown hair became entangled in a bush, she kept walking, the bush tugging at her hair like thin fingers, only reluctantly letting go.

"They're following," came Sarika's whisper from behind.

Molly glanced back. Although none could be seen, much less heard, she thought that all the animals of the forest were crowding behind them, making sure they didn't retreat from Tessa's determined lead.

The deeper they went into the forest the wilder it became. The town and Mum's farm and anything at all human seemed like on another planet.

No one could live here in the wood, not with all nature against them. People did not belong here; humans were not wanted. If Mr Fanshawe were to build all his houses the people in them would still not belong. They never would. Some places were not intended for people.

At one point Tessa vanished and Molly heard a splash. A moment later she stumbled forwards down a small bank and landed in water. A small shriek burst from Sarika as the same thing happened to her.

It was the stream that flowed through the wood. Tessa waded across and the girls followed, and behind came the faint sounds of water as other animals followed them. Molly needed both hands to climb out the other side. Her shoes and the bottom of her jeans were soaked, and her sleeves up to her elbows. The water seemed even colder than before.

At last Tessa stopped. Molly and Sarika drank from their water bottles, and with her hands shaking Molly couldn't help spilling some.

"We shouldn't have come," said Sarika. She stayed close to Molly, and kept glancing over her shoulder at the darkness behind.

"Yes, we should," replied Molly. "This is the true forest. Tessa wanted us to see this." But the raw, feral menace of the place crept under her skin. They were lost, and at Tessa's mercy, for only she could lead them out again. If Molly gave in just a little, if she let the fear go just a little deeper into her mind, she would start crying. And she would not let that happen, not in front of Sarika and certainly not to herself.

"The animals." Sarika looked all around them. "They've gone."

"No," said Molly. "They're just very still. This place—I know it now."

They were in Obidee's secret bower. In the darkness it seemed very different, more oppressive, smaller. They had come by a different route than before, avoiding the road. But there was no doubting the small ring of stones—she could just see them through the gloom.

"Obidee?" she called. And then, because she knew he'd never liked the name, "Only-By-Darkness?"

Human language was as alien here as humans themselves. Tessa shivered a little at Molly's words, but none of the dozens—or maybe by now it was hundreds—of animals around them, took the slightest bit of notice.

Molly pulled her hand back as something touched it. Just a leaf: no, leaves, lots of them, falling from the branches above them and onto the two girls. The wind stirred through the trees, and the leaves fell.

Molly brushed the leaves away, but Sarika said, "No. It's deliberate."

"What do you mean—oh!"

The leaves swirled about them in the wind, in their hair, brushing against their faces, flicking across their vision. And yet the branches of the trees stayed still. The wind no longer stirred them, just the leaves. And how could the wind do that, here in the bower, where all else was still?

"The trees don't want us here either," whispered Sarika.

Molly gulped and reached for Tessa's lead, but the dog moved away to the other side of the bower and sat down, watching them with her large liquid eyes.

"Only-By-Darkness," said Molly again. "Stop teasing us. If you're here, show yourself. We have to talk. We see now what you mean about the forest. We're trying to stop the development, we really are. But causing damage and hurting people isn't going to work. It's just..."

She stopped.

A light had appeared far away between the twisted branches of the trees. A soft, orange light, wavering slightly.

Immediately the animals stirred, making noise now as they moved back and forth. Something small but fast darted along the ground. The long, sinewy form of a lizard slid over one of the rocks. Behind her, the grunt of a wallaby.

"What's that?" asked Sarika, pointing at the light.

"I don't know."

It wasn't Obidee. Someone else in the forest, someone with a torch. One of the construction workers, perhaps. At that moment a sound came to them, like a large vehicle moving through the trees. The light must be the headlights.

"They're going to cut the forest down tonight!" said Sarika. "We have to stop them."

The animals continued to move away. The swirl of leaves stopped and it seemed to Molly that the tree branches moved away, as if shying from the light. They felt wind again, not cold now but warm against their flesh.

How mean of Mr Fanshawe to start the destruction of the forest in the middle of the night, as if ashamed to do it in the day. But it meant the death of the forest had started.

Just then Molly heard the unmistakable sound of a car engine starting and moving away.

"Over there!" she said, as two headlights shone almost directly into their faces. "Let's get after him!"

Without another word, or even another thought, Molly plunged into the forest. She turned her torch on as she went, not heeding the undergrowth now, not caring where she put her feet, just trying to close the distance between her and the car.

The other light, glowing now a bright orange, continued to shine.

Molly stopped when she reached the road. The car had gone, but ahead of her, a few metres off into the bush, was a fire.

CHAPTER 15

THE BURNING HEART

Molly stared at the fire, struck dumb and motionless by the sight, the heat bathing her face and hands. As yet the blaze was confined to a bush and a small area of grass, but a nearby stringybark tree would soon catch. In the dry undergrowth the fire would spread faster than it could be extinguished.

What to do? The fire was already too big for her to put out by herself, but she took off her jacket anyway and started to beat the flames. It did little good, and soon Molly was driven back by the heat.

"Oh no!" screeched a voice. Sarika emerged from the trees, hand to mouth, her eyes reflecting the firelight.

"Help me!" panted Molly, and for another minute the two girls beat at the fire. But no good: the stringybark tree caught alight, the flames igniting the dry bark like paper.

"We have to get help!" called Sarika.

"Along the road! Quick!" Molly started off in the direction of the destruction site but only went a few steps before she turned. Sarika hadn't moved.

"Come on!"

"We can't leave the fire."

The flames had already moved to another tree, climbing up in ribbons of orange and blue.

"There's nothing we can do. Come on!"

But to leave the fire, to just let it burn—the whole forest would catch alight, and all the trees and animals would die. Besides, Tessa had run off somewhere. No way would Molly leave the dog to burn to death.

The tree emitted a deafening bang like a gunshot as the flames engulfed it. Sarika picked up her jacket and beat at the flames, but dropped it when one sleeve caught alight.

"Oh, I've just made it worse!"

She put her hands over her face, either to shield it from the heat of the fire or to cover her shame. Molly ran back and hugged her. "Come on, Sarika," she said. "There's nothing we can do. We have to…"

Another light appeared in the forest, a long way off up the road.

Another fire. A bigger one by the look of it, somewhat closer to the farm, if Molly had her directions right.

Something touched her foot. She glanced down to see a long form sliding over her shoe. A grass snake. Molly didn't even try to flick it off, just let the creature slither away from the flames. Around them, the forest came alive as animals started to flee the fire. They have more sense than we do, thought Molly, as a wallaby bounced past. Overhead a bird flapped between the trees.

Then Molly heard another sound above the crackle of the flames. A car engine. And there, up ahead, the forest was lit for a moment by two car headlights further up the road.

"Come on," Molly called, but this time she headed towards the car.

"Where are you going?" asked Sarika.

"Someone is starting these fires deliberately."

They hurried along the road, the darkness coming back once more as they left the first fire behind, the sound of its hungry feast on the trees fading away.

Molly was about to flick her torch back on so they could see the dirt road ahead of them when a bright object leaped out from the bushes.

Obidee.

An utterly changed Obidee. He stood hunched over, as if cowering, and on his face a look of abject terror. His bristly hair was hanging loose now, and the leaf-like clothes he wore were browned and dry. He clutched his hands together and looked at the two girls with large, liquid eyes.

A moment after, Tessa emerged from the same spot. She ran to Molly to rub against her leg, but kept both eyes firmly on the sprite.

"There you are!" cried Molly.

Obidee scowled, the corner of his mouth twisting up. "Your dog brought me." The sprite turned away from Tessa a little, as if about to run.

"Don't try it," warned Molly. "Tessa can run faster than you, even through the scrub. She's a hunting dog."

"I know! I'm not going to run." He glanced at the second fire, pointed a scrawny, twiggy hand at it. "But see what's happening."

"There's another one along there," said Sarika. "Did you do it?"

Obidee reared up, all fear gone, as he spun on Sarika. "You think I did this? You think I would set fire to my own forest? Stupid girl!"

"Don't call me stupid!" barked Sarika, drawing herself up and placing both hands on her hips. "I'm not stupid."

"We have to do something," put in Molly, trying to bring the talk back to more important things. "Obidee, can you put the fire out?"

"No. And the more we stand here talking about it the worse it gets."

"So what do we do?"

"I'll run for help," said Sarika. "I can cut through the forest. Obidee can guide me."

"No!" hissed the sprite. "I'm not leaving the forest while there are animals caught by the flames."

Molly said, "It's a good idea, Sarika. Tessa can guide you. Get back to the farm and phone the fire brigade."

Sarika gripped Tessa's leash, her face set in a determined frown. "All right."

"Home, Tessa!" Molly commanded. "Go home, girl!"

The dog wrinkled her nose in the smoky air, then lowered her head and stalked off into the undergrowth. Sarika, clutching the dog's leash, stumbled after her.

"Hurry!" roared Obidee, then coughed as the smoke grew thicker.

Sarika and the dog disappeared into the darkness. Molly had a horrible thought that they might lose themselves in the wood despite Tessa's homing instinct, but forced the idea out of her mind.

Obidee hopped about on the road as he regarded the two fires, one before and one behind.

"This is madness," he said.

"Never mind that." The smoke had grown thicker. "What do we do now?"

The sprite grinned. "So, you want to do things my way now? You're not going to just hold up a sign saying 'Put the fire out'?"

"What do you...? So you did do the damage at the destruction site."

"Yes. I'm strong when I need to be."

Molly found it hard to imagine the little sprite, less than half her own height and literally as thin as a stick, tipping over a bulldozer or hauling the giant fallen tree across the path. But she knew nothing about who he really was, or what strength he might summon if needs be.

"All right. Tell me what to do," pleaded Molly.

But Obidee hung his head. "We can't do anything. The fire is already getting out of control."

Molly started running towards the second fire. She had no idea what she would do when she got there, but couldn't just stand around. Perhaps an idea might occur to her when she arrived and saw the situation.

It didn't take long to get to the second fire, and it was worse than the other. A car was parked there, both headlights on but the engine off. Beyond it the flames burned fiercely in a small hollow surrounded by gum trees and thick bushes. The hollow was blazing, the flames already taller than Molly. Sparks flew high into the air, landing on the trees, or floating away into the night to settle outside the hollow. Soon this whole part of the forest would be alight, and in no time it would sweep to the edges, and leap to the houses beyond, including her mother's farm, perhaps even reach the town itself. She watched the fire in stupefaction, feeling light-headed.

Obidee had faded in the bright light of the fire, but could still be seen as a wavery form, like a flickering mirage. He tugged at Molly's leg. "I have to help the animals out. Come with me. We can't do anything here."

Obidee was right. Sarika might be able to reach a phone and call the emergency services, but by that time the whole of Hallow's Choice might be gone.

A glowing ember landed at her feet and the grass and dead leaves there instantly ignited. She stomped on the tiny flames and ground them out, but another ember landed near Obidee and did the same thing. He cowered away, retreating behind Molly's leg and clutching at her.

"It'll burn me," he whimpered.

Obidee was made of wood, or something very like it.

Molly forced herself to think. Every instinct told her to run—and yet she could not will her legs to move.

"The animals," she said. "We have to—"

Something moved in the hollow. Not flame, not leaves stirred by the rising heat, but the movement of something living. An animal trapped in the fire.

Then Molly let out a gasp. Not an animal—a person.

Distinctly framed against the burning trees was a human figure. It stood in the centre of the blaze, looking about. As Molly watched it tossed away a small metal can. The blaze of the fire, the dense smoke, were too great for her to distinguish if the figure was a man or woman.

"Someone's in there!" she cried, but as she said the words the figure vanished as smoke swirled between them. When the smoke cleared, no figure could be seen.

Obidee had moved further away, back to the car, cowering under it. Embers and sparks dropped around him.

She took a step towards the ring of flame, then fell back as the heat seared her face. No good. She took her backpack off and rummaged in it for the bottle of water, splashed some into her eyes to clear the soot and dust, and peered once again into the raging inferno.

There! Again, the figure, this time on the far side of the hollow, up near a big tree. But even as Molly watched it tumbled backwards and lay still.

She had to help them. But how? She couldn't enter the flames, and even the smoke was wrapped around her, groping with grey fingers. She fought a weird compulsion to push the smoke away.

Coughing, spluttering, she retreated to the car.

"There's someone trapped!" she cried to Obidee.

"Who cares? Let's get away and save ourselves."

In that moment, Molly hated Obidee. Ava at school was nothing to the sprite. She was a bully, but had her limits. Obidee was a bully, too, in his own world, but not being human Molly had no idea how to deal with him.

And no idea how to save the person trapped in the hollow.

Again she stepped towards the flames, arm held across her face, peering against the horribly bright light. But the flames drove her back again. In the light of the fire Obidee was barely visible under the car. Only his eyes stood out clearly, reflecting the orange firestorm.

More trees exploded into flames. A burning branch fell, almost hitting Molly. Hopelessly, she tried to stamp on it, but it was too far gone to have any effect. Leaves under the branch burst into flame.

"We have to run!" urged Obidee.

Molly shut her eyes. The urge to run, the instinct to tear off down the road, became overwhelming. She forced herself to look back towards the first fire. It had already spread across the road, cutting them off in that direction. No retreat. Where did the other end of the road go to?

Every bit of common sense told Molly to run along the road, to flee the fire that was now out of control. But even as she watched, a tree on the other side of the road caught embers blown by the wind, and the upper branches crackled into flame. The fire now straddled the road in both directions.

They were cut off.

I'm going to die, she thought. The idea made her shiver despite the overwhelming heat of the fire. "No. I won't let that happen," she said out loud.

"What?" Obidee's voice had become a high squeak.

Molly had had enough. She'd had school, and she'd had Hallow's Choice and she'd had enough of having to live on the farm and she'd really, really had enough of this little sprite who acted all tough and mean, but who folded up like a piece of paper when things were against him.

She reached under the car and hauled the sprite out. His clothing rustled and his skin felt like dried paper. "No! Don't!" he screeched.

"Be quiet!" roared Molly. "Now you're going to help me. We're going to rescue that person in there and then escape."

But the sprite pushed at her hand with such strength she let go with a squeal of pain. "He did it!" roared Obidee. "That man in there! He must have set the fire. It's his fault."

"That doesn't matter. He'll die if we don't rescue him. No one deserves to die."

But Obidee crossed his arms and shook his head.

Molly's heart sank. No way of getting through the flames now, no way to save the person trapped. If she didn't run she, too, would be unable to escape. Even the bare earth of the road felt hot through her shoes. The air came burning hot into her lungs, mixed with smoke. She could not stop coughing.

But the person inside the flames. How to save them? Could she drive the car through the flames? She'd never driven a car, didn't even know how to do it. But maybe...oh, there had to be something.

She ran to the driver's side door and wrenched it open. The air in the car smelled so good, so pure. Molly knew the inside would be a sanctuary from the fire. The petrol tank would not explode, and she would be able to breathe as the fire passed by, but still she couldn't bring herself to climb in.

Too bright now for her to see the sprite. The flames lit the world as bright as day, and Only-By-Darkness had become invisible.

"Obidee!" she called again, just in case. No reply.

Then she noticed, on the edge of the fire-filled hollow, a dead bottlebrush tree. For some lucky reason the flames had not yet reached it.

"Obidee!" she screamed. "We need to push that tree down!"

No reply. Molly ran to the tree and shoved her whole weight against the trunk. Like trying to move a mountain. The roots, although dead, still kept the trunk firmly attached to the ground.

But if Obidee had pushed over that tractor at the destruction site, he must be able to do something with this skinny tree.

Again she pushed, and a moment later had to fall back, her face dripping sweat, mixing with her tears. No good. Nothing was any use. The trapped man would die and so would she, and nothing was any good ever. She collapsed on the burning ground and cried.

"Out of the way!" called a voice.

Molly felt herself shoved aside. Things crawled on the ground around her. At first she shrank back, wondering what horrors had come out of the ground. When something ran across her face, tickling, she flicked at to try and knock it away.

"Get out of it!" said the voice.

Molly looked at the bottlebrush tree. It was vibrating. The whole trunk leaned a little and then sprang back, the few remaining branches knocking against each other. Soil around the tree's roots was being flung aside by some unseen means. Then the tree vibrated again, and this time when the shaking stopped the whole tree leaned a little—just a little—further towards the hollow.

"Give us a hand, then!"

At the base of the tree was Obidee, barely visible, his form shifting in and out of sight as the flames flickered. He had set himself against the base of the bottlebrush and was pushing hard. Molly stood and put her hands against the trunk further up.

"I've dug some of the roots out," cried Obidee. "Now, push!"

Molly pushed with all her might and the tree moved a fraction.

"Again!"

Another huge push and Molly felt she would burst. But the tree leaned a little further towards the flames.

"One more!" the sprite roared and together they pushed like never before. Molly felt her heart would leap out of her chest as she put all her strength into shoving at the trunk, and Obidee at her feet heaved too.

At last, with a huge crack and a spurt of soil from the snapped roots, the tree toppled into the flames. Already the fire had consumed the grass and bushes in the hollow, leaving scorched, blackened earth. But the trunk now made a safe path over the still-burning embers, a path that almost reached the still figure at the other side of the hollow.

Molly didn't hesitate. She stepped onto the trunk and used it as a bridge to cross over, both hands out to keep her balance. She tumbled off at the other end, putting her hands on the ground to stop her fall.

She screamed in pain. The ground was burning hot. She jumped to her feet and hugged her hands under her arms. But even in her pain she focused on what she had to do.

She reached down and hauled at the trapped person. His clothes were scorched, his hair singed from the fire. Ash and twigs clung to his face but they didn't stop Molly recognising him.

It was Mr Fanshawe.

She gasped in surprise, but that just made her cough again. She hacked away for a moment, and came back to reality.

Beside Mr Fanshawe lay an empty can, and on the can was written, Kerosene.

"Obidee!" she called, but no reply came.

Mr Fanshawe coughed and his eyes opened, filled with horror. He looked at Molly.

"Who?" he said. "What?"

"No time," replied Molly. "Can you stand up?"

"Yes. I think so. I must have been knocked out when I fell."

He put his hands down to stand up, and cried out when the burning ground scorched them as it had Molly's hands.

Molly let him lean on her as he rose to his feet. "Come on," she said, "we have to get away."

They went back along the tree trunk, but when they emerged at last at the other side, Molly groaned. She had let the door of the car open, and the fire had engulfed the interior of the vehicle. The seats were burned and the inside a smoking ruin. The last act of the fire as it roared off to consume the rest of the forest. No escape that way.

"We have to go along the road," said Molly. "It's still burning on either side, but we could make it if we're lucky."

"This way," said Mr Fanshawe, hobbling along. But he only got a few metres before he fell. He coughed hoarsely.

Molly hauled out her water bottle and put it to Mr Fanshawe's lips. "Here." He gulped at it, but it just made him cough again.

They couldn't walk, so they crawled, Molly leading, Mr Fanshawe behind, clutching occasionally at her foot. The first time she shook him off, but after that let him grab her foot as it assured her he was still there.

It took ages to crawl along, looking out for falling branches. The forest was burning fiercely on either side now, no trace of the night left, the sky glowing orange and red. Smoke roiled across the road.

After a long time, just before Molly was ready to give up and lie down forever, her hands encountered something hard, but not part of the road.

A metal bar.

She looked up. The bar was part of a sign, and through her burning eyes she could just make out the words, "Hallow's Creek".

The creek! They could shelter there. Molly rose to her feet and went a few careful steps further. Sure enough, the road dipped down and forded the creek.

"Come on Mr Fanshawe!" she said, and leaped down into the water. The road went under it and emerged on the other side. There was no bridge, but the water ran less than knee depth.

The sudden change in temperature made her giggle. "Come on Mr Fanshawe!"

But the man had collapsed. Molly waded out back to him. "You have to get up. I can't pull you. You're too heavy."

He looked up at her, face smeared with dirt and soot so only his teeth shone white as he grimaced.

"I can't," he moaned.

Molly clenched her fists. "If I can, you can, a big grown man like you."

He managed to clamber to his feet and together they went the few metres to the creek. He rolled into the water and lay there. Molly lay down too, relishing the coldness.

It revived her wonderfully. She scooped up handfuls of water and gulped them down. Her parched throat reacted and she coughed most of it up again. But it satisfied her burning thirst and she lay there, letting the water wash through her hair and clothes and take all the heat away.

She decided she might live after all.

But still the inferno raged about them. The low, steady roar of the fire filled the air, a king who would not be overruled, an unforgiving master that destroyed anything and anyone who dared to stand against it.

Looking up into the trees that arched over the creek, Molly

imagined she was back in her bed in the farm, the plastic stars above her glowing in the night. On her desk was the globe of the world, and it was spinning, the continents and oceans a blur, as if tempting her to stop the spin with a finger, to point out a place, any place, that she might be rather than here. The vision seemed to last for ages.

Someone touched her. She sat up, water cascading off her. "Obidee?"

But there was a man standing over her, a man dressed in a yellow jacket and over-pants, with a white helmet on his head.

"Are you all right?" he asked.

"Yes...No...Mr Fanshawe..." She turned to where Mr Fanshawe had fallen into the creek.

"He's all right," said the man. "Come on, let me help you up."

"Who are you?" Molly asked. She had the absurd notion that the man was going to carry her off to somewhere on the other side of the globe. But the stars had stopped shining above her, and the spinning globe was nowhere to be seen.

"I'm from the fire service," said the man. "Come on, we're not out of this yet."

CHAPTER 16

CHOICES

When Molly presented herself at the hospital ward the nurse scowled. "He's not supposed to see any visitors."

"Oh. But he asked me to come." She clutched a bouquet of flowers in one hand.

The nurse looked down at a clipboard on her desk. "Well, I don't have anything here."

"Molly saved his life," said Mum proudly, but it still didn't seem to make any impression on the nurse.

"I'll have to check with the police," persisted the nurse.

Just then a police officer appeared at the desk and said, "It's all right. This is Molly Travers."

The nurse still didn't seem to like the idea, but let Molly and her mother go through into the room where Mr Fanshawe lay in bed, propped up on pillows, with bandages on his face and hands. The police officer followed them in and sat down on a chair by the door.

Molly wondered how Mr Fanshawe might greet her. A little cautiously, she said, "Hello, Mr Fanshawe."

"Hello, Molly."

The flowers weighed heavy in Molly's hand. "I brought you these," she said, holding them out.

The bandages on Mr Fanshawe's face moved as he smiled. "Thank you, Molly."

Her mother found a vase and took the flowers to place them in it. "How are you?" she asked, and Molly blushed because she realised that was a question she should have asked herself already.

"Mending," came the short reply. "Molly—you saved my life. Thank you."

Saved his life—the words struck Molly deep. The blush in her cheeks went redder, but at the same time her heart thumped strongly in her chest.

"I only did what anyone else would have done," she said. "But please—why did you set the forest on fire?"

Mr Fanshawe glanced at the policeman, who raised an eyebrow.

"Did I say something wrong?" Molly looked at her mother.

"It's tricky, Molly," said the police officer. "The reason I'm here is because Mr Fanshawe has been arrested for arson— that's the crime of burning property. The whole town could have been destroyed. So, while he's here in hospital recovering, he's also in custody until his trial."

"At which I've already told you I intend to plead guilty," put in Mr Fanshawe. "But it might be better, officer, if you remained outside the door for a moment?"

The policeman smiled. "All right. But don't try and escape while I'm outside, eh?"

Molly thought the relationship between the policeman and Mr Fanshawe most extraordinary. If he was under arrest, shouldn't he be in handcuffs or something?

After the policeman had gone, Mr Fanshawe said, "He's respecting my right to silence. But I'll tell you: I set fire to Hallow's Choice because I wanted people to lose interest in protecting it. I thought that if it no longer existed as a forest, you wouldn't be so concerned about it, and I could go ahead with building my houses. Except..." He moved a little on the bed, and it seemed to hurt him.

"Are they giving you something for the pain?" asked Mum.

"It's all right. Thank you. Except I didn't factor in the idea that anyone might get hurt. Including myself. I was too liberal with the kerosene. The first fire was fine, and I went on further to light the second. But it got away from me. It's a good thing you turned up when you did. I would have died there."

Again, Molly's heart thumped so loud she wondered if the others could hear it.

"I shouldn't have been in the forest either," admitted Molly. "I was trespassing."

"And a good thing too."

"Trespassing, yes," put in her mother. "And doing silly things when they should have been in bed, going off without telling anyone. She's in a lot of trouble."

Molly winced. When Mum had found out about their adventures, she had been livid. Molly was grounded almost for life, and yet in the middle of her anger, her mother had on a couple of occasions expressed pride in Molly's actions in saving Mr Fanshawe.

"I believe there was another girl," he said. "Is she all right?"

"Yes. Sarika got to the farm in time and they called the fire service."

"I'm glad."

Poor Sarika had had a terrible journey through the forest. She bore several bad scratches and had once fallen down a short slope of rocks. At another point in her journey, a metre-long snake had slithered away just as she was about to step on it. But Tessa had led her steadily onwards, and they managed to reach the farm and wake up Mum. Sarika was also in trouble from her parents, but Molly was sure they, too, felt pride in their daughter's bravery.

"So what happens now?" asked Molly.

"So now I go to prison for a while." The smile went away from Mr Fanshawe's face. "But I deserve to. You didn't just save my life, Molly, you changed my mind. I can see now what a selfish fool I've been. I won't be building the housing estate now."

"But if you don't build there," said her mother, "someone else will. The Council will just find another developer."

"I've been talking to some people in the government," said Mr Fanshawe, shaking his head. "I know one or two politicians who owe me favours, you see. And they're going to have

Hallow's Choice declared a national forest. No one can build there ever again."

Molly's mouth opened in astonishment. This meant they had won! Obidee and the animals were safe. The fire had been extinguished in time so only part of the forest had been burned, thanks to Sarika's promptness. But the rest was still there. The burnt part would grow back in time.

But Obidee had vanished. Had he been killed or injured in the fire? Molly certainly wasn't going back to look for him. The forest was well and truly out of bounds now.

Would she ever see the wood sprite again?

***

The Loser Tree looked a little greener on the first day back at school after the holidays. The branches that hung almost to the ground had new shoots on them. The grass surrounding the twisted roots grew more thickly. Molly imagined the tree stood up a little straighter, as if proud of her, or less miserable about itself.

As if sensing the change, other students no longer went to the tree during school breaks. But Molly and Sarika made it their regular haunt. They ate their lunch sitting under the low branches, feeling the breeze on their faces. The weather had turned cooler in the last few weeks.

They had talked a few times about their adventures, and wondered what had happened to Obidee, but as time went on, they talked less about him. It seemed he had moved on, or always stayed now in the damaged forest. Or—and Molly didn't like to think about this—he had not survived the fire.

But one gloomy, cloud-filled day, when most of the students stayed close to the school buildings because of the threat of rain, Molly and Sarika ate their lunch as usual under the tree.

Molly had just taken a bite of her ham and tomato sandwich when she paused, teeth still firmly in the bread, and squinted at a small bush just outside the school fence. It was shaking when there was no wind.

"Look there!" she said, and Sarika pulled the water bottle she had been drinking away from her mouth.

"What?"

And there was Obidee, hardly visible in the daylight, just a smear of colour, and quite transparent, but unmistakably Only-By-Darkness himself. He came to the chain-link fence and put his hands out to grip the wire.

Molly leaped up. "Obidee! I'm glad to see you!"

But the sprite merely shrugged. "Are you?"

She looked at him carefully. He seemed uninjured. Molly realised she had been looking for signs of injury—burn marks, maybe, or even some parts of the sprite burned off, like a tree might be damaged by fire.

"Of course I am."

Sarika joined Molly. "And I'm glad to see you, too," she said.

"Where have you been?"

The sprite shrugged. "In the forest, where else? Trying to repair things. Many animals were injured by the fire. This is the first time I've been able to get away."

"Well, it's a good thing you weren't hurt." Molly choked a little, "I was afraid…"

"Of what? That I'd died? No. Sprites are smarter than people. I managed to get away. But I was angry with you."

"With me? Why?" Molly had received praise from everyone for saving Mr Fanshawe's life. A representative of the fire service had come out to talk to the whole school about fire safety in the bush. And the Mayor of Moolooran had presented both Molly and Sarika with awards for bravery. Molly's certificate now hung in a frame on her bedroom wall. To have Obidee say he disapproved of her actions came as a bit of a shock.

"You saved that monster who tried to kill us all," the sprite said. "That Mr Fanshawe."

"I did what I had to do," retorted Molly. "You'd have…"

She stopped. She had been going to say Obidee would have

done the same, but knew that wasn't the case.

"I did help you," said the sprite. "I didn't want to, but I did. And you taught me a lesson. My ways—damaging property, hurting people, even trying to kill them…Yes, I admit. I wanted to push that girl under that car—my ways didn't work. Your ways did."

"Mr Fanshawe has changed his mind about the forest," said Sarika.

"So I gathered. All his equipment has gone."

"And the government is going to make it a national park, so no one will be able to build anything," put in Molly. "It'll remain forest always."

The sprite put his hand through the wire mesh. Molly took it between two fingers and felt amused when Obidee formally shook her hand exactly as if he were human. "My ways didn't work. Nature is a wild thing, and humans need to appreciate that. But you can't talk to someone in a language they don't understand."

"So, you're going back to the forest now?" Molly felt choked. "We aren't—aren't going to see you again?"

Obidee squeezed her fingers. "Of course you are. You're both welcome to come and visit me in the forest whenever you like. But don't expect to always find me. I've got a lot to do. But I'll be there, even if you can't see me."

"We can hardly see you now," said Sarika, giggling. "Why are you only visible in the darkness?"

"That's my nature," said the sprite. "Darkness. Badness." He smiled and stuck his tongue out. "Evil." He drew the word out in an overly dramatic way. "But maybe not as evil as I once was. Or maybe—maybe I'm more tolerant of good."

"Well, that's a relief," said Molly.

"I've made my choice," said the sprite. "I could continue being bad, I could become good. I might end up in the middle."

"Mr Fanshawe made a choice too," said Sarika. "A good one."

But suddenly the sprite wasn't there. Whether the sun had

come out from behind a cloud or for some other reason, he had vanished away.

"Obidee?"

But there came no reply.

"He's wild," said Sarika. "He comes and goes as he pleases."

Just then a voice spoke from behind them. "What are you two doing?"

Molly and Sarika threw glances at each other as they recognised the voice.

Ava Penfield.

They rose and turned away from the fence. "Nothing," said Molly. What did nuisance Ava want?

But she saw that her fears were unjustified—even a little cruel. The cast had gone from Ava's arm, which was all healed now. The girl stood alone, with no bully friends like Katie and Grumpy to back her up. And she was smiling. Molly could not remember the last time she had seen Ava smile warmly, not in the stuck-up, superior way she usually did.

"Poking about in the bushes?' said Ava, but there was no hint of malice in her voice. Just genuine curiosity.

"I thought I saw a mouse," said Sarika.

"Oh. I wanted to talk to you two."

And Ava, for the first time ever, sat down under the Loser Tree. Molly and Sarika approached despite the misgivings that still clung to them.

"I haven't spoken to you since school started again," said Ava. "I was too embarrassed. But—you saved my uncle's life. The whole town knows it. And they know what a bad thing he did."

"Well…" began Molly, but then kept quiet.

"I was terrible to you. And to a lot of other students. But I've made a choice now to try and be better. I nearly died!" She touched her arm. "And I realised that my uncle was a big influence on the way I behaved. So, I wanted to say sorry for all the things I did, and thank you."

"That's fine, Ava," said Molly. "Thank you. And yes, we

quite forgive you."

"That doesn't mean we're friends!" A scowl appeared on Ava's face, but it lacked the old arrogance and menace. "But you know what I mean."

"Yes, we do."

Ava stood up and walked off back to the playground. Molly looked back at the fence and the bush, but Obidee did not return. Not even the faintest shadow remained of him, and somehow she knew that he truly wasn't there, that he had gone back to his beloved forest.

"He'll be back," said Sarika.

"I know," said Molly. "He'll always be there now."

ABOUT THE AUTHOR

Russell Proctor is an Australian writer, teacher and actor. Besides writing, he likes bushwalking, astronomy and cats. He enjoys travelling to out-of-the-way places and has climbed Mount Kilimanjaro in Africa and walked the Kokoda Track in Papua New Guinea. He has written a number of novels and short stories, but this is his first for children.

www.ingramcontent.com/pod-product-compliance
Lightning Source LLC
Chambersburg PA
CBHW071313130626
46556CB00004B/1599